GIVE ME SOMETHING GOOD TO EAT

GIVE ME SOMETHING GOOD TO EAT

D. W. Gillespie

DELACORTE PRESS

Text copyright © 2024 by D. W. Gillespie
Jacket art copyright © 2024 by Matt Ryan Tobin

All rights reserved. Published in the United States by Delacorte Press, an imprint of Random House Children's Books, a division of Penguin Random House LLC, New York.

Delacorte Press is a registered trademark and the colophon is a trademark of Penguin Random House LLC.

Visit us on the Web! rhcbooks.com

Educators and librarians, for a variety of teaching tools, visit us at RHTeachersLibrarians.com

Library of Congress Cataloging-in-Publication Data is available upon request.
ISBN 978-0-593-65181-0 (trade) — ISBN 978-0-593-65183-4 (ebook)

The text of this book is set in 11.5-point Caslon Pro.
Interior design by Jen Valero

Printed in the United States of America
10 9 8 7 6 5 4 3 2 1
First Edition

Be warned . . . this book is full of monsters.

It was written for kids who love monsters,
and it was dreamed up by me, a lifelong admirer of monsters.

It's dedicated to Grant and Lily,
my two favorite monsters in the world.

CHAPTER 1

The Best Night of the Year

It was Halloween in Pearl, North Carolina, and the normal rules of the world didn't apply. Abbie Purdom was only six years old, but even she understood that. Her mother, Beth, had spent the day getting the house ready for the festivities. It didn't matter if you didn't enjoy handing out candy or if you preferred not to decorate. There was only one way to celebrate in Pearl. It was an invisible contract you signed the day you moved to town. Everyone participated. No one sat out, at least no one respectable. If you lived in this town, you were in, all the way.

This was the first year Abbie's mother let her pick out her own costume, and she settled on a very cute bee with a plastic stinger sticking out of the bottom. Now that she had it on, Abbie couldn't stop staring at herself in the mirror, wiggling her butt.

"Oh my gosh," her mother said. Beth was dressed as a sunflower, and she held up her phone to record her daughter as she pranced around in front of the mirror.

"I'm gonna sting you!" Abbie screamed as she chased her mom around the bedroom.

"You can't sting me," Beth said, scooping her up. "I'm your momma flower." They squeezed each other tightly. "I love my little bee *so much*."

"I love you too, Momma."

The sky was purple when they stepped out the front door into the chill air. Orville Avenue was a living kaleidoscope of color and lights, like a child's daydream come to life. The metamorphosis of the town that had begun in early September was now complete, and a skull-faced butterfly had hatched, ready to fly.

The unspoken rule of Halloween night was simple: the little kids went first. The street was pulsing with activity. Big, gaudy skeletons, inflatable dragons, and giant spiders dotted every yard they passed. Abbie's eyes glowed when she saw them. The bee and the sunflower fell right into the line of people heading east toward the town square, stopping at every house they passed to load up on candy. Soon, the little bee could barely hold her bag, and Beth had to carry it for her.

"It's too heavy," Abbie said.

Beth winked. "Well, I'll help you out with that."

They both dug in, and in a few moments, they had eaten a dozen pieces of candy between them.

"We should take it easy," Beth said as she dug another piece out. "Then again . . . it *is* the best night of the year."

The sky was nearly dark now. The teenagers were starting to emerge, the princesses and knights replaced by zombies with spilled, dangling guts, groups of girls shrieking and taking selfies in animal onesies, and grim reapers with blood-slicked machetes. Pumpkins glowed from every stoop, some silly, but most with toothy mouths filled with jagged teeth.

"Momma," Abbie said, leaning into Beth.

"It's okay . . . it's all for fun."

They gave up on getting more candy and walked to the middle of town, cutting across Orville Avenue and into the tangle of alleys that separated it from Main Street. The alleys were a common shortcut for people walking to the square, but Abbie never liked them. The brick buildings were so close that the sky always narrowed to a slit. It made her feel like she was walking into a dungeon. Abbie huddled ever closer to Beth as they passed a couple of grown-ups who kissed and laughed and smelled like beer. The pair separated just long enough for Abbie to see the woman's face, which was painted red.

"Happy Halloween, little *bee,*" the devil woman growled as they walked past. Abbie buried her head into her mother's waist and refused to look up until they were out of the alley.

"Hey, we're through . . . check it out."

Abbie looked up and saw Pearl Park, a wide span of lush grass and gigantic willow trees contained within the town square. The rectangle of grass was surrounded by a footpath and a quiet street lined with old-fashioned storefronts. Coffee shops, sandwich stores, and pizza joints threw open their doors and pulled tables out onto the sidewalk for Halloween.

For one night only, everyone ate and drank outdoors. Dogs on and off leashes chased each other across grass, dressed up like devils and hot dogs. In the center of the park was the Fountain of Bacchus, a massive pool of dancing water with an enormous classical statue in the center. As she always did, Abbie perked up when she saw it.

"Who's that?" she asked, giggling at the almost naked statue.

"Bacchus. He's the Greek god of . . . well . . . partying."

The statue itself was ten feet tall and perched on top of a pedestal that stood over twelve feet tall. The bronze had gone green over the years, but Bacchus's frivolous grin remained undimmed and he tirelessly held his cup aloft, as if raising a toast to the world.

"He's not wearing clothes," Abbie said with another giggle.

"I know, baby."

They made a full circle around the park, just so the pair of them could see the decorations. The hanging willows were draped with purple lights, and ghosts hung and swayed in the breeze. Even with all the laughter and music, the scene was surreal and unsettling, and Abbie realized she was quickly getting her fill of Halloween. They turned the corner at the far end of the park and headed back home, passing the cemetery. It was the only part of town that wasn't decorated, a detail that somehow made it more chilling. As they walked silently past it, the wind picked up, and Abbie shivered.

"Momma."

"It's fine, baby. Just a cemetery."

Just then, a couple walked under the streetlight a few feet in front of them. It was a cheerleader and what looked to Abbie like a caveman.

"Beth, is that you? Oh my God, you are so *cute*!"

Abbie had seen this scene unfold plenty of times. Her mother would catch up with her friends on, well, pretty much everything, and Abbie knew she wasn't going anywhere soon. She began twirling around her mother's legs in little circles, humming to herself to pass the time. She kept her eyes on the cemetery, which was now half a block away. Far enough to be safe, but still too close to not keep an eye on.

She made a circle around her mom's legs, once, twice, a third time. It was the fourth time that she stopped when she saw a young girl standing in the shadows of the cemetery. She was dressed in a black sweatshirt, its hood pulled up over her short black hair. Her skin was as pale as milk, and her deep-set eyes looked almost purple in the reflection of the street-light. It was impossible to tell her age. She could have been as young as eight or as old as seventeen. For a moment, the dark-haired girl stretched and yawned as if she were awaking from a long nap. Then she turned to Abbie and smiled.

Abbie scrambled back behind her mother's legs and buried her face in Beth's thighs.

"Easy, Abbie, Momma is talking."

When Abbie finally worked up the courage to look once more, the dark-haired girl was still standing there, still smiling. The only difference was she had something in her hand, a small doll that she held aloft. Squinting at it, Abbie took a step away from her mother. The strange girl held it in front of her, shaking it like a dog toy, and when Abbie had taken a half dozen steps forward, she recognized what it was.

The doll was simple, probably handmade from the look of it, with a sweet, plump, smiling face. Yellow and black stripes ran down its body. And at the bottom was a stinger made of felt. The doll was a bee, or more accurately, a little girl *dressed* like a bee. The dark-haired girl noticed that Abbie had finally figured it out, and her smile deepened. Abbie was afraid and confused but seeing that smile put her at ease.

She stepped forward, hands outstretched.

"Stay close to your mom," the dark girl whispered, but her voice sounded like she was speaking directly into Abbie's ear. Even stranger, Abbie never saw the girl's mouth move.

"Come on, Abbie," Beth said, scooping her up from behind.

"But, Momma, the doll . . ."

She pointed back over her mother's shoulder, but the girl and the doll were gone. Mother and daughter continued on, tracing their way back through the square, back down the alleys, and back onto Orville Avenue, which was wilder than ever. After being bumped by people left and right, Abbie realized her mom had finally had enough.

"Ugh . . . baby, you gotta walk a little bit."

Beth slipped Abbie down to the sidewalk and they eased back against a fence, out of the foot traffic, which was heavier than ever.

"Momma's got to rest for a second," Beth said, catching her breath. "We're almost home, but we walked farther than I thought we did."

Abbie was only distantly aware that her mom was talking. Instead, she was staring through the wrought-iron fence at the house behind it. Like all the yards in town, it was packed with decorations, but one of them stood out. The centerpiece was an eight-foot scarecrow made of sticks and roots and draped with a long black jacket. The eyes in its jack-o'-lantern head glowed with a strange green light that seemed to pour out over the jagged teeth. The scarecrow looked too real somehow, not like a cheap decoration at all, but real wood and a real pumpkin with real, unearthly fire bubbling inside it.

"Scary scarecrow," Abbie whispered.

Beth glanced back and yawned.

"Yeah, it is. . . ."

The wind was soft, the night was suddenly cold, and Abbie kept on staring at the scarecrow, certain that if she looked away, even for a moment, it would come to life. Even the sound of the noisy partyers seemed to die away, and Abbie felt strangely alone, as if the only thing left in the entire world were her and the scarecrow.

"Mommy . . ."

In the roar of the crowd, Beth never heard her daughter's voice. Instead, she watched the passersby for a moment before fishing her phone out of her pocket. It was already almost ten o'clock.

"How did it get so late?"

Time always did seem to move weirdly on Halloween, especially since they'd moved to Pearl.

"Five minutes!" someone yelled.

The mob around them roared. It was nearly time for Pearl

to carry out one of its oddest traditions. At ten o'clock on the dot, every pumpkin would be snatched off the porches, dragged out to the middle of the street, and smashed to a pulp. Orville Avenue would become Orange Avenue. It was a wild example of shared madness, and though the people were laughing, Beth always found it unsettling, as if the entire town were suddenly under some kind of spell. No one objected, regardless of how detailed their jack-o'-lanterns might have been. Every single one would be pulped into the concrete. When the morning came, the entire street would be orange with pumpkin guts.

"It's almost time for them to smash the pumpkins," Beth said. "You fell asleep last year. You remember that . . ."

She glanced down. Abbie was gone.

"Abbie . . ."

Beth scanned the yard of the house behind her, sure that her daughter was getting a closer look at the decorations, but she was nowhere to be seen. Neither, Beth realized dimly, was the towering scarecrow. Frantically, she turned back to the street, to that frothing ocean of people flowing in every direction.

"Abbie!"

She tried to stay calm, but she couldn't, not when that wall of ghoulish faces passed by, laughing and grinning with blood-soaked fangs, wild eyes, and clawed hands.

"Abbie!" she screamed. "Help!"

"Two minutes!" someone yelled, and the crowd split and divided, rushing to grab the nearest pumpkin, to be ready for the moment of triumph.

"Help me!"

Fear had hold of Beth now, and in the frenzy, she felt a gentle hand at her shoulder. She turned and saw it was Ms. Vernon, the kind old woman who lived a few houses down from her. She mostly kept to herself, and she struck Beth as rather odd. Even so, she always smiled and waved at Abbie when the two of them walked by. She was wrapped in a blood-red cloak with a spiderweb pattern on it and holding a cane with a gruesome face carved into the end. To Beth's surprise, there were also spiders in her hair.

"Ms. Vernon! Please . . . you have to help."

"Help with what, dear?"

"Abbie! She was right here, and now . . . now . . ."

"Oh, honey," Ms. Vernon said sweetly. "You're fine. You're *safe.*"

"No, Abbie . . . we . . . we have to find her."

Beth heard a clicking sound, and she realized that Ms. Vernon was tapping her strange cane on the ground. One, two, three times.

"I . . ."

Ms. Vernon was whispering as well, though her voice was far too soft for Beth to make out the words.

". . . I have to find her . . ."

Ms. Vernon finished her nearly silent words.

"Find who, dear?" she asked.

Her smile was simple and knowing.

"I . . . have to . . ."

"Have to what?"

The young mother opened her mouth to speak, but only a single word emerged.

". . . find . . ."

"There's no one to find," Ms. Vernon whispered. "After all, it's Halloween. It's the *best* night of the year."

Beth's eyes were watery, and a tear worked its way free and spilled down her cheek.

"The best night of the year," she whispered, repeating the words like a robot.

"That's right. And look . . . they're about to smash the pumpkins! You should be out there, joining in the fun."

Beth's face changed from a fearful grimace to a wide smile. Only her eyes still held pain and terror.

"You're right," she said, her voice full of childish excitement.

Ms. Vernon's eyes were warm, and her smile was comforting. One of the spiders in her hair twitched, but Beth didn't notice. She was overwhelmed with a sense of peace, the way she had felt when her mother tucked her into bed so many years ago.

"No need to worry about Abbie, is there?"

Beth tilted her head.

"Who's Abbie?"

"Ten seconds!" the crowd yelled.

"Don't you worry about that," Ms. Vernon said. "Go on, enjoy yourself."

Beth walked away on shaky legs, out into the middle of the street. The people of Pearl, young and old, screamed and hollered as they began to paint the asphalt orange with pumpkins. She laughed and joined in, stomping a half-smashed jack-o'-lantern to bits. She was dressed as a sunflower, though for the life of her, she couldn't figure out why. She was crying too, but she couldn't figure that out either.

There's nothing to be upset about, she thought as the pumpkins rained down on the pavement like hail. *After all, it's the best night of the year.*

Across the street, a lone figure didn't join in the mad pumpkin smashing—it was a boy in a hockey mask who wore a pair of black plastic glasses on the outside of the mask. He was looking at Beth, studying her carefully. Without taking his eyes off her, he slipped off his glasses, slid up his mask, and put the glasses back on. His straight black hair draped down into his face, and he brushed it aside as another boy appeared next to him.

"Mason, you not smashing any pumpkins?" his much-taller friend asked.

"No," Mason said quietly. "Serge . . . we gotta talk."

CHAPTER 2

The Kid Who Remembers

"Broadly speaking, spider venom falls into two main categories," Mr. Burkitt said. "Neurotoxins disable the nervous system, making it easier for the spider to wrap up and transport its prey. Necrotoxins, on the other hand, actually kill the tissue around the bite area. You most commonly see this type of bite in humans with the brown recluse. In humans, some extreme cases can cause the skin around the bite area to rot away. The effects can last for months. . . ."

It was Halloween, exactly one year after Abbie Purdom went missing, and Mason Miller couldn't concentrate on his seventh-grade science teacher or how various types of spider venom worked. A spider lecture should have made for a great day, especially considering that it was Halloween and a Friday. He should have been excited. Only he wasn't.

"Now, on to feeding. After wrapping up an insect, the

spider doesn't eat it. Rather, it expels digestive enzymes into the insect, liquifying it so the spider can *drink* the insides."

Mason perked up. Even as distracted as he was, this was a wonderful detail. An image of a common garden spider came up on the screen behind Mr. Burkitt.

"Here is a garden spider. Totally harmless to humans, but . . ."

The words began to roll off Mason once again. Even gory spider mayhem wasn't enough to keep him focused on the lecture, not today. It was the day that he and his best friend, Serge, had been talking about for months. The town was ready, as always, to celebrate Halloween, but they were all blind to the mortal danger lurking, waiting.

Not Mason. He knew too much.

Last Halloween, Abbie Purdom, a kindergartener, disappeared.

The Halloween before, it was Riley Sapp, a boy in third grade.

And the Halloween before that, Terrell Barr.

And so on, through the years, an unbroken string of names, stretching back too far for any grade school kid to remember. And worst of all, not a single grown-up ever acknowledged that the kids were missing. Instead, it was like an awful game of telephone, the word passing from kid to kid, trying to figure out who was taken this year, but for some reason, only Mason seemed to care for more than a week or two. Eventually, even the kids just seemed to . . . forget.

Mason always felt a guilty sense of relief come early

November when he heard that it wasn't anyone he knew. But this time was different. Abbie was so young, only six and only in school for a few months, that it felt unfair. A third grader could run, could scream, could put up a fight, at least.

The only question was, a fight against what?

Worst of all, Mason had been there, *right next to Abbie's mom* when it happened. He could still remember the way she screamed and freaked out, only to suddenly stop and pretend like nothing was wrong at all. But the scary thing was, it hadn't seemed like she was pretending.

Mason felt the same way he did whenever he read his old books about the Bermuda Triangle or Stonehenge. This town had *secrets*, and he wanted to be the one to uncover them. If not for himself, then at least for the younger kids.

The bell rang, and he jumped, knocking his books to the floor. A few kids around him laughed, but he didn't hang around to hear any of their comments. He was the first one out the door and into the busy hallway.

Serge was leaning on his locker, waiting for him, and when Mason saw him, a familiar thought came into his mind.

He's so much cooler than me.

Not that there was anything particularly wrong with Mason. He was a little shorter than most kids his age, but not drastically so. His hair was dark and hung over the top of his glasses just far enough to make him flick his head a thousand times a day. He was mostly the type of kid you could walk past without really noticing, a pale shadow on the wall, easily missed and just as easily forgotten.

Serge was Mason's opposite: short hair, a chiseled, dark-brown face, and broad shoulders he'd built from lifting weights with his dad the past year. He was well on his way to being the best player on the middle school football team. As if that weren't enough, he was also near the top of the class in grades. He was one of those kids who was good at almost everything without even really trying.

"So, what's the plan?" Serge asked as Mason threw his books into his locker.

"For what?" Mason asked.

"For tonight!"

Mason looked around, making sure no one was close.

"I'm thinking don't die is a pretty good plan."

"I honestly don't think you're gonna die."

"Keep your voice down," Mason hissed. "This is *deep cover* stuff. We have to be careful."

Just then, a group of football players swarmed past, and Mason stuck his head in his locker, avoiding them.

"What's up, Serge?" a wide slab named Greg asked.

The football players slapped hands and banged their chests together, all in one smooth motion. To Mason, it seemed quite unnecessary and even a bit painful. Once they were gone, he slammed his locker door.

"Every one of those meatheads could be part of the conspiracy," he said. "We don't know who we can trust."

Serge sighed. "Sometimes I wonder why we're friends.

You are literally the most paranoid white dude I've ever met, and that's saying something."

"No one understands the danger around here like I do," Mason said, his voice rising. "Not even you, and if I have to do this by myself, then—"

"Did you listen to what I just said?" Serge asked. His voice was calm and even, which always drove Mason nuts when he was getting angry. "I said you're my *friend*. You don't have to do anything by yourself."

Mason thought back to when the two of them had first started hanging out years earlier. It was Mason's first season of soccer. One season was all it took, and despite the sprained ankle, the sunburn, and the bee sting in the center of his forehead, it hadn't been a complete waste. He'd come out of that rough spring with a new friend, at a time when he really needed one. He and Serge had zero in common, besides scary movies and video games, but somehow they clicked.

"Fine," Mason said. "Here's the plan. My house at three—"

"Let's get something to eat first."

"Fine, my house at three-thirty—"

"Can we get Benson's?"

"I don't really feel like burgers."

"Dude, I need the protein."

Mason readjusted his glasses and let out a prolonged *ugh*. "Okay. Benson's right after school. My house at three-thirty—"

"I need to get the bat from my house."

"I thought you brought it. You're supposed to be dressed like a . . . baseball guy or whatever."

"I'm going as Mookie Betts," Serge replied. "You know? Plays for the Dodgers?"

"I'll take your word for it."

"Either way, they don't let you bring bats to school."

Mason took a deep breath and closed his eyes.

"Well, we *do* need the bat for protection," he said. "It's a key part of the plan."

"Yeah . . . *plan* . . ."

Mason ignored the sarcasm. "So, let's try this again. Leave school. Get *burgers*. Get your *bat*, and *finally* get to my house."

"When's that?"

"Who the crap even knows at this point. . . ."

"Let's get to class, boys," a familiar voice boomed. Mason glanced back and saw Vice Principal Kirby, his eyes hidden beneath the square shelf of his forehead as he strode down the hall.

"My bad," Mason said with a nervous laugh.

Vice Principal Kirby was, as far as anyone knew, the only person in town who didn't participate in any of the Halloween festivities, a profound act of defiance that most people wouldn't even consider. No one had ever seen him smile, and there was a rumor going around that he actually *couldn't* smile.

As he lumbered past, the vice principal murmured something about not getting paid enough for this job.

"I'm not saying I believe you," Serge whispered after he was out of earshot. "But if your . . . *theory* about this town is true, Kirby is involved. He's just gotta be."

"Look, he for sure seems like a guy who would kidnap a bunch of kids, but it's just too obvious."

"I heard he's like a survivalist or something. My dad says he saw him at the sporting goods store buying ammo."

"Like I said," Mason replied, "he's too obvious. If you want to crack this code, you gotta see what's hiding under the surface. It's never the guy you think it is. You have to start with the people you wouldn't expect."

"Not everything has to be some puzzle for you to figure out."

Mason held a hand to his chest as if he'd been wounded. "What does that mean?"

"I mean it's just a thing you do. When we're watching a horror movie, you try to figure out who's the bad guy nonstop. You can't just *enjoy* anything, you know? You can't just be in the moment. My dad was actually listening to this podcast on mindfulness, and—"

"Wait," Mason said, holding up a frustrated hand. "We can't skip that last part. Do I try to figure out movies? Yes, I do. Sue me. It might come in handy someday."

The bell rang, and they sprinted down the hall.

"To be continued," Mason said.

"See you in the lobby at three," Serge called as he disappeared into the crowd. Mason stood for a moment, thinking about everything he knew and everything he hadn't been honest with Serge about. It was time to come clean, to finally let his best friend know the real reason he was so convinced their town was cursed. It was like there was some spell on this town that affected everyone, even Mason.

The only difference between him and everyone else was the notebook.

Without looking, Mason slipped a hand into his backpack and drew the notebook out. Its pages were turning yellow by now, and he had to keep it together with a thick rubber band, but the notes were there, written clearly in number 2 pencil. He checked it daily, sometimes to scribble new notes about a potential subject and sometimes just to remember. Despite his obsession, at that very moment, Mason could feel the memories becoming hazy and vague in his mind, but once he saw the notes and their *names,* it all came roaring back. He was convinced that the notebook was an anchor holding the memories in his mind, keeping them from drifting away in the currents.

"Mr. Miller," a voice said behind him. He turned. Vice Principal Kirby strode back down the hall. "Do you see anyone else in the halls?"

"Nope. I was just on my way to—"

"Maybe that should be a clue for you. There is no one left in the halls because class is about to—"

The bell cut off the end of his sentence, and Mason smiled. "I'm on my way."

"Watch yourself, Mr. Miller," the vice principal said. "I worry that you might be the type to wander out into the woods, *never to be seen again.*"

"Uh, wow, I'll, um, keep that in mind."

Mason spun around to walk away, and as he did, he saw a metal clip on Vice Principal Kirby's pants pocket. He couldn't be completely sure, not without stopping and staring, but he could have sworn it was the clip of a pocketknife. Mason carefully put the notebook in his backpack.

Had the vice principal just threatened him? Mason swallowed, then shook his head. Nah. He'd just watched way too many horror movies.

CHAPTER 3

Mason's Notebook

"Okay, so Saitama versus Superman, who wins?" Mason asked. He and Serge were walking through the school lobby on their way out the door and into the sunny autumn day that awaited them. Mason had succeeded, as he often did, in dragging his best friend into a deep philosophical conversation, usually regarding which fictional characters would win in a fight.

"Why are you asking me?" Serge replied. "You're the one with all the details of every character memorized."

"I have *my own* answer, but I'm just curious what . . ." Mason paused, gazing over Serge's shoulder. "Oh, great."

"What?" Serge asked.

"She's out there again."

Serge turned to see for himself. Becca Rosen was sitting on the brick half wall, her best friend, Mari Ito, beside her.

"Dude, it's like every day for a week," Mason said, not bothering to hide his annoyance.

Serge grinned. "I mean, it's not the worst problem in the world."

Mason took a deep breath and held it for a moment. There was little doubt that Becca was waiting in that exact spot for a reason. Serge and Mason walked past it every day, and each time they did, she got a little braver. The glances had turned into grins and finally bloomed into awkward small talk.

"All right, you stop and say hi, but then we've *got to go*," Mason said. "We've got a schedule to keep."

"Yeah, yeah, yeah," Serge said as he led the way, leaving Mason to follow along, feeling like a third wheel.

Becca's face lit up as soon as she saw Serge.

"Hi, Serge!" she yelled a bit too loudly. Mari, who seemed, like Mason, to be a mere bystander in the scene, shrank back, no doubt out of embarrassment. Becca smiled, apparently immune to any sort of shame.

Becca and Mari couldn't look more different. Mari had straight black hair, always pulled back and out of her eyes, while Becca had a head full of wild blond curls and dimples on each cheek.

"Uh . . . hey, Becca," Serge said with an easy smile as he stood a bit taller. "So . . . how's it going?"

His voice was totally changed now, deeper, like he was doing an impression of his dad. Mason grinned and had to look away to keep from laughing, and when he glanced back, he saw that Mari was doing the same thing.

So, it's obvious to her too, he thought.

"It's good," Becca answered. "Are we going to see you guys out tonight?"

Serge cut a quick glance back at Mason, who shrugged.

"Yeah," Serge said. "We'll be out and about. You just got to keep an eye out for a sharp-looking baseball player and . . ." He looked at Mason again. "What are you going as?"

Mason rolled his eyes and sighed loudly. He hated trying to explain himself, especially when it came to horror, because none of the kids his age ever seemed to get his references.

"I'm going as Ash."

Mari crinkled her eyebrows. "Like, from Pokémon?"

"What? No!" Mason shot back. "He's the main character in the *Evil Dead* series. He fights monsters, says cool lines—" He broke off, not wanting to explain his choice.

"My boy here is all about old horror movies," Serge said. "I keep telling him he needs to start a YouTube channel."

Becca smiled. "Really? I'm not into stuff like that. But who knows . . . maybe we could hang out and watch something spooky sometime?"

Mason's eyes nearly rolled to the back of his head, but Becca didn't notice. Mari cupped a hand over her mouth, and Mason knew she was struggling to keep from laughing.

"Okay," Mason said as he began to drag Serge away, "we're in a pretty big rush. Got a lot on the *agenda.*"

"So, we'll see you tonight?" Becca asked.

"Yes," Mason said. "I'm sure we will."

"I'll keep an eye out," Becca said as Mason and Serge walked away. "For a cute baseball player and . . . the other guy."

They walked for about a minute in silence, with Mason, both annoyed and anxious, glancing back occasionally to make sure they weren't being followed. "So, what's the deal with Becca?"

"What do you mean?"

There was a defensive edge in Serge's voice that Mason didn't like.

"Nothing. Let's get something to eat at Benson's."

Benson's Diner was an institution in Pearl, especially among the middle school kids who walked home in the afternoon. The burgers were cheap, greasy, and of questionable grade. Mason preferred the fries slathered in nuclear-orange cheese sauce. The place was cleared out, as everyone in town, including Mr. Benson, was preparing for the night's festivities. It wasn't until Mason and Serge sat down with their food that their conversation picked back up.

"So, about Becca," Mason said as he nervously tapped his foot. "It's nothing against her."

"Why would you have anything against her?"

Mason picked at a basket of cheese fries while Serge devoured a triple burger with cheese. A cardboard cutout of a bat hung down between them, swaying back and forth in the breeze from the open door. Mr. Benson was already dragging chairs out onto the sidewalk, and each time he passed, he gave the boys the stink eye, silently demanding they hurry up.

"I mean, it's Halloween," Mason said. "She seems . . . cool, but we've been planning all year for tonight. It's literally the most dangerous night to be a kid in this town."

Serge burped. "What's that got to do with her?"

"Exactly! We don't have time to . . . I dunno, watch her flip her hair."

Serge rolled his eyes. "Hey, if she was flipping her hair at you, you'd want to hang out with her."

"Well . . . I . . . just . . . whatever."

"Look, the plan is still on, all right? We're going to be on alert. Checking the crowds out. Seeing what's going down." Serge took a huge bite, wiped the grease off his mouth, and then, after a thoughtful pause, said, "I know this whole . . . deal means a lot to you. But how do you know?"

"Know what?"

Serge set down his burger and shook his head.

"Look. You know I got your back. It's just . . . your *theory* seems impossible. Kids don't just disappear without anyone noticing. I mean, I sort of remember the rumors from last year—about that girl in kindergarten—but they can't be real, right? The cops would be knocking on every door on Orville Avenue. CNN would be in our front yards. And even if it is all true, why are you the only one that knows for sure?"

"This again?" Mason said as he reached for his backpack. "I told you I got notes on everything."

"I remember. *The notebook.* It doesn't really prove anything, and even if it did, why you? Why are you the only kid who would think to write down all this crazy stuff?"

Mason felt his heart begin to thump, its pace quickening. *Go ahead,* he thought. *You've come so close a dozen times. It's Serge. Go ahead and tell him.*

"All right," he said gravely. He dug into his backpack and drew out the notebook before snapping the rubber band off

25

it. "After I tell you this," he said with utter conviction, "you'd *better* be all in!"

"Fine. I promise."

Mason leaned in closer, waited for Mr. Benson to walk out of earshot, and then opened the notebook. "Take a look at this." He pointed. The writing was crude, clearly the work of someone very young. Serge squinted at the words, which were in faded pencil.

"'The Monster That Ate the World,'" Serge said, but the title was written as *The Monstir That At the Wirld.*

"Look at the next line," Mason said.

"Written by Mason Miller and . . . it's all smudged out."

"Exactly." Mason leaned in even closer.

"Does the name Marco Diaz ring any bells?" he asked.

"Not that I know of."

"Before you moved here in third grade, he was my best friend. Who am I kidding, he was my only friend. He was the first person I had a sleepover with. I learned to swim with him in Mrs. Glenna's swimming class. We used to sneak horror movies from his dad's collection and watch them in my room. This kid was *real.* Those memories are *real.* And this notebook? We wrote this story *together.*"

"I don't get it."

"I don't either. He disappeared on Halloween in second grade, but as far as this town knows, Marco never even existed."

"What do you mean?"

"I mean I told my mom he wasn't at school. I'm not joking

when I say that this kid spent the night at my house like ten times. *She said she'd never even heard of him.* Said I was making him up. She even went so far as to threaten me, saying she'd take my video games or movies away if I kept lying. I felt like I was going crazy, man."

"Dang," Serge said quietly. "I can't believe you never told me."

Mason felt a sick clenching in his gut and a sour taste in his mouth. He'd never talked about any of this before, and now that he had started, there was no stopping, no matter how tough it was. He looked down at his plate, deeply regretting the cheese fries.

"It's worse than you think. I checked my old class yearbooks. *Nothing.* Marco just vanished. I was about to force myself to admit he wasn't real, that I was just having some kind of multiyear dream that I suddenly woke up from. And that was when I remembered our story."

Mason held the notebook.

"It was still there, but his name was smudged. Every day for a week, I kept checking it, and it got more and more faded until . . . it was just *gone.* And that's not even the worst thing—"

Mr. Benson appeared next to them, seemingly from out of nowhere, and Mason clamped his mouth shut.

"You boys need anything?"

"Nah, we're good," Serge said.

"You know, boys," Mr. Benson said impatiently, "we're moving all these tables and chairs outside for Halloween."

"We're almost done," Mason said. "The fries are really good."

Mr. Benson snorted and walked away.

"We gotta get going," Serge said.

"Mr. Benson can wait." Mason's heart was thumping. "I've tried to tell you this so many times, so I've got to get it out. The worst part was Marco's mom."

He took a deep breath as if readying himself for what he had to say.

"My mom and I bumped into her at the grocery store. It was probably a month after he'd gone missing. I remember it was right after Thanksgiving. All the Christmas stuff was out. I think Mariah Carey was playing . . . not sure why I remember that. I was so excited when I saw Marco's mom. It was like my last chance to do something. My mom stopped and talked to her. They actually remembered each other!"

Mason was back there, back in the store with the music playing and the decorations hanging overhead, so excited to see some proof of his friend's existence.

"I just kept staring at her, waiting for her to look at me, and when she did, I blurted it out. 'Why hasn't Marco been in school?' She just stared at me for a minute. Then she smiled and asked, 'Who's Marco?' My mom just laughed it off. Said I was in a very *imaginative* stage. And after that, I knew."

"Knew what?"

"Knew there was something *very* wrong with this town. Knew that I had to try to fix it somehow."

He flipped a few pages past the story and then stopped.

The words on the new page were darker and clearer. "I took out this notebook, and I started writing the same thing over and over. 'Marco Diaz was real.' For like five pages, just the same thing over and over."

"Like that dude in *The Shining.*"

Mason smiled and wiped his running nose. "Good reference."

"When I got you for a best friend, it's hard not to pick up some things."

"Yeah. And that's why Marco was my buddy too. He showed me my first scary movie, some old DVD we stole from his dad back when we were little kids."

Mason smiled, lost in the memory.

"It was the first time I'd ever seen an R-rated movie. It was old. The effects were so goofy and gory. But I loved it, and Marco loved it, and that's why we were buds. And now he's part of a very exclusive and awful club. I got a list of them now. Names of kids I never knew, friends of friends, little brothers and sisters, cousins. This town just swallows them up. Last year, I was so close to it. I saw Abbie Purdom's mom losing it, and then two seconds later, she was smashing pumpkins and laughing. I wish I didn't know all this, but I *do*. So I've got to try to do something."

Serge pushed his basket away. It was the first time Mason hadn't seen him finish a meal in a while.

"I can't believe you never told me about your friend," Serge said.

"I wanted to tell you everything last year, but I couldn't. It was hard enough to tell you about Abbie."

Serge laughed, but there wasn't any humor in it. "I'm sorry, man. I wish I'd known earlier."

"I figured you'd think I was crazy. Everyone else does."

"Like I said, you know I got your back."

The relief that washed over Mason was stronger than he could have imagined.

"You don't have to give me a hug or anything," he said, picking at his fries and trying not to get too worked up. "But yeah, I mean, that's why I told you."

With a deep, shaky breath, he ate one last fry before clearing the table and following Serge outside. No more than thirty seconds later, Mr. Benson came out the front door with the table they'd been sitting at. Mason stretched and gazed out at Pearl Park and the giant marble fountain in the center.

"This place will be packed in a few hours," Serge said.

"That's right," Mason said as they started walking. "I got your back too, you know?"

Serge smiled, the way you might smile at your grandma when she says you're the biggest, strongest boy in school.

"I know."

"I'm serious, man. I mean . . . I'm not as fast as you. Or as strong or whatever. And you're way better at math than I am. But . . . I still got your back."

"I *know*," Serge said.

With that, the two of them made their way toward Orville Avenue and toward the night that would change them and the town of Pearl forever.

CHAPTER 4

The Plan

Orville Avenue was almost impossibly straight, with barely a hill or a bump. You could stand on one end and see almost clear to the other end, past dozens of blocks and hundreds of houses. Some of the homes were quite large, with big, wide-open lawns and plenty of space. On the far west side were the oldest houses, smaller, humbler, but with huge trees that made it feel like you were walking straight into the woods that swaddled the town.

Mason and Serge lived on the west end of Orville Avenue in a neighborhood with lots of families with lots of kids running around the streets. It was a short walk, and despite how nervous he was, Mason felt electrified. It was Halloween, the air was crisp, and anything could happen. They stopped by Serge's house for him to change and grab his bat while Mason waited outside. He loved Serge's parents, but if he made an appearance, they would end up burning half an hour just catching up. Tonight, there wasn't any time to waste.

"We gotta hurry up, man," Mason said when Serge reappeared in costume. "Night's falling soon. And with the night *comes the darkness.*"

"Who are you, Batman?"

"This is serious, dude. This is our chance to finally get to the bottom of all this. To save this town. To defeat whatever kind of evil is happening here."

"Defeat evil?" Serge asked. "So dramatic."

"Okay, so maybe it's not quite so big, but still. We're going to be the only ones looking for anything weird. If something happens, maybe, just maybe, we can stop it."

They walked in silence for a moment, and then Mason pushed his glasses up on his nose and added, "And yes, I'm like Batman."

The pair passed the oldest section of Orville. The buildings here were all red brick. Some of them were apartments, and lots of them had been converted from old businesses that had gone under years before. Everything in this section felt lived in and historical, and Mason loved cutting through the alleys behind the old buildings—it was like he lived in an actual city instead of a tiny, hidden town nestled in endless woods. As he picked up his pace, Mason caught Serge slowing down and gazing up at one of the square brick buildings.

"What is it?"

"I think Mari lives there," Serge said.

"There?" Mason gazed up. "Weird house." There was a door at one corner, and he tried to figure out the layout of the place in his head. If it was an apartment, it must be almost completely vertical, with three floors stacked right on top of each other.

"It's kinda cool," Serge said. "Like living in a loft or something."

"Why are you so interested in Mari?"

Serge laughed. "Just wondering if Becca might be there."

"I doubt it," Mason said, feeling a stab of annoyance. "Becca lives out on Mayfair, right? Everyone in that neighborhood drives cars more expensive than my house. She's probably too fancy to come to this side of town very often."

"She's not like that," Serge said. "I mean, she's rich, but—"

"Dude, you got all night for . . . all this. Let's pick up the pace."

"Whatever. I'm faster than you on my worst day anyway."

To prove his point, Serge took off, leaving Mason to huff and puff after him. When Mason finally reached his house, Serge was sitting on the back porch waiting for him.

"Took you long enough."

They came in through the back door, and by the time they hit the kitchen, they heard the yell.

"Maaasonnn."

His little sister, Meg, came around the corner. She was nine years old, but to Mason's endless annoyance, she was starting to get tall. The generally accepted fact was that she would catch her brother by the time she hit junior high. She was currently dressed as a Disney princess, though which one Mason couldn't begin to guess. As soon as she saw that Serge was with her brother, her eyes lit up.

"Hey, Serge!"

"What's up, little princess?" he asked. She ran over, preparing to give him a hug, when Mason stepped between them.

"What?" he asked in his most annoyed big-brother voice.

"Mom says you have to take me out trick-or-treating."

"That'll be the day," he said under his breath.

"Excuse me, young man!"

Mason turned around and saw his mom standing in the hallway. Jen Miller was as short and solid as a fire hydrant, and her usually friendly face was twisted into a furious grimace.

"I . . ."

"You what?"

Mason sighed, and decided honesty was the best approach.

"I didn't know you were standing there."

Meg grinned, showing off the missing tooth she had lost a few weeks ago. She had her brother's dark hair, but it was a long, shimmering black veil over her shoulders. She wrinkled her freckled nose at Mason, who sneered back.

"Well, Mr. Smart Guy, you're taking her out with you tonight," his mother snapped.

"Why?" Mason yelled. "We've got plans for tonight."

"Plans," his mother scoffed. "What are you doing? Meeting the mayor? Doing your taxes? You can take your sister trick-or-treating."

"Mom, I haven't been trick-or-treating in like *two years.*"

Serge was giggling, and Jen smiled at him. "Mason's dad and I are going over to your house for a cookout, Serge, so hopefully you two can take her for a lap up and down the street."

"Can't she just go on her own . . . ?"

Mason trailed off, realizing what he was suggesting. His sister was a huge pain in the butt most of the time, but he loved her. Even if their mom let her go out by herself, Mason couldn't just stand by and do nothing. If something bad happened to her, he'd never forgive himself.

"Fine," he said. "We'll take her down the street and back."

"Both sides!" Jen wagged her finger.

"Ugh . . . fine. But after that, we're dropping her off at Serge's house."

"That's fine." Jen straightened up and looked at Serge. "So, what do you boys have planned after that?"

"Just hanging out. Probably meeting up with some friends."

Jen smiled at Serge.

"Some *girls*?"

Serge grinned back.

"I mean, I can't speak for your son—"

"Yes!" Mason yelled in his most annoyed tone, the one he saved for moments just like this. "There will be girls there. Can I go get ready now?"

"Yes, Mr. Grumpus. Go get dressed."

Mason and Serge passed the living room, where Mason's dad, Sam, was sitting in the recliner and drinking a beer.

"What are you boys up to?"

"Just about to go out. With *Meg*, apparently," Mason grumbled.

"Mmm," his father grunted. "You got any trouble planned?"

"No."

"Serge? Any trouble?"

"No sir."

"Y'all are boring," he said. "You should get into at least a little trouble."

Mason sighed. "Sure thing, Dad."

"I'm just messing with you," Sam said, taking a long sip of beer. "Be careful out there. Don't stay out too late."

Once they were inside his room, Mason shut the door and shook his head.

"Okay, so taking Meg out changes our plans a bit," he said. "But we can at least keep an eye on her."

"Good thinking," Serge said. "Plus, it's half an hour to make the trip, tops."

Mason sat down on his bed and sighed. "When I was little, I always thought it was the coolest thing in the world to live in a town like this. I mean, look at all this stuff." He motioned to the walls, which were papered with posters of horror movies: *Halloween*, *It*, and, of course, *The Thing*. A small desk sat in one corner, but it was barely big enough to hold a laptop with all the figurines that covered it. They were divided into neat little groups: the slashers, the classics, the aliens, and the giants like King Kong and Godzilla. They were like Mason's second little family, which watched him sleep every night.

"Who knows?" he said. "Maybe that's the reason I love all this stuff. You grow up in a town obsessed with Halloween, what else can you do?"

Serge was twirling his baseball bat and sinking into a

crouch, as if awaiting a pitch. "I dunno. Maybe play sports. Start looking at colleges."

"Ew," Mason said. "Who wants to do that?"

Serge laughed. "You overthink things, man."

"Maybe it's not me. Maybe everyone else *under*thinks things!"

"Maybe . . ." Serge pulled the desk chair out and sat down across from Mason. "Either way, *you* would have still been *you* in a normal town. It's just who you are. And besides, you're probably the only one who could have figured out what was going on here."

Mason couldn't help but smile. He'd never considered the idea before, but maybe all his quirks, all his *weirdness,* was a sort of superpower if you looked at it from a certain angle.

"Never really thought of it like that," he said.

"It's not a bad thought," Serge said as he pointed at the rows of toys with the baseball bat. "Maybe all this is *exactly* what makes you the right person for the job."

Mason smiled again. The suggestion that he was the right person to fix Pearl was a wonderful thing to consider, but he also knew the truth: without Serge's encouragement, he might have found a way to talk himself out of it.

"All right," Mason said, slapping his knees. "New schedule is, we get Meg, sprint up and down Orville, drop her off, then start walking the streets and keeping our eyes peeled for anything suspicious. Your phone charged?"

"Of course."

"Perfect. The key to this whole thing is to *document* it.

We'll take pictures *and* videos of anyone shady. We might forget stuff, but our phones won't."

"Right."

"And if we see anything, we'll stop it. Get some parents involved. Whatever it takes." Mason took a deep breath, as anticipation for the coming night, in all its dangerous glory, filled him, tingling along his spine. "All right . . . baseball guy."

"Mookie Betts."

"Whatever." Mason smiled. "It's time to go to work."

After a few quick pictures and a warning to "keep an eye on your sister," Mason, Serge, and Meg set off into the darkening evening. Mason was now officially in costume as Ash, *not* from Pokémon but from the horror movie *Evil Dead 2,* complete with one sleeve torn off his blue button-down shirt and a holster across his back that held a toy sawed-off shotgun. No one would get the reference, at least no one his age, but that was part of the point. Mason understood it, and Marco would have too. That was good enough.

The air was already growing cooler, and a sharp October breeze filled Mason's lungs, pumping him full of energy. Meg, dressed as a princess with a glittering tiara, walked between him and Serge until they stopped at the first house on their route. Mason kept his eyes on Meg the entire time.

"All right, so I spilled my guts to you," Mason said as Meg walked up the lawn toward the elderly couple who lived there.

"But why do you want to solve the mystery of Pearl now that you know more of the story?"

Serge frowned. "Like I said, I got your back."

"Okay, but say we run into a serial killer, and we have to fight him to the death. What'll keep you going?"

Meg came back down the lawn, and they paused the conversation for the twenty seconds it took to make it to the next house. Once she was gone again, Serge said, "It doesn't have to be some grand thing, you know."

"What's that mean?"

"It means you can do something good just because it's good. Life's not a movie. I don't need to have some epic emotional arc."

"Fine," Mason said. "You're just a good guy then. Probably *lawful good* in D&D terms. Maybe a barbarian or something."

"You're just mad 'cause I put all my points in charisma," Serge said with a grin.

"You see what I'm saying, though. It's different for you. The stuff with Marco messed me up, but there's more to it. I don't expect you to understand, though."

"Hold up," Serge said, brow furrowing. "What exactly does that mean?

"Hang on a second," Mason said as Meg returned. "Did you tell them thank you?"

"Yes, *Mom*," she said with a roll of her eyes.

Mason reached into her bag and grabbed the first piece of candy he could find. It was one of those orange wrapped peanut butter mysteries. He hated them, but he popped it into his mouth on principle.

"Hey! That's mine!"

"It's called the big-brother tax," Mason said, chewing loudly and trying not to grimace. "Get used to it."

Meg huffed and ran up to the next house. There were more people on the street by then, but the crowd was still barely scratching the surface of what the place would look like in another hour or two.

"You were saying," Serge said.

"Look, you've played sports your whole life, right?"

"Yeah."

"So, when you were like eight, you probably heard fifty people cheering for you as you rounded the bases. When you were ten, you were scoring touchdowns. Even now, you're already making the junior high stadium scream. You know what I got? I took a year of piano lessons, and at my first recital, I peed my pants and ran offstage."

Serge laughed. "Aw, I remember that."

"Thank you for your concern," Mason answered. "My point is, I'm not like you. I haven't done anything worthwhile yet, but maybe, someday, I'll do something interesting with my life. Maybe I'll make a horror movie and hear people cheer at a film festival. Or maybe I'll write a screenplay that wins an award. Or maybe nothing like that will ever happen. Maybe I'll stay here and work at the mustard factory."

"They pay good. My uncle works there."

"That's not the point! I don't want to make freaking mustard. I want to do something cool, something where I'm the hero, you know? Figuring out what's happening here, and stopping it, could be my first step in that direction."

40

Meg walked up, this time holding her bag close to her chest.

"Get anything good, you little wiener?" Mason asked.

"Are all big brothers like you?" she huffed.

"Yes. I checked. I talked to every big brother in the world, and they all said their little sisters were wieners."

Meg ran off once again, and Serge turned to Mason, his face serious. "Just so you know, you don't have to be good at football to be a hero for somebody. You should ask Meg about that sometime."

Mason felt a snarky response rise up in his brain, but he decided to leave it there. They continued down the street, and Serge's message, much to Mason's annoyance, stuck with him, rattling around his head as they walked. For the next few houses, Mason didn't say anything, but he watched Serge joke around with Meg, digging around in her bag for any candy that she didn't want.

"Hey, I'm hungry," Serge said when she pushed him back.

"You're always hungry."

A few minutes later, they came to the first street that sliced into Orville Avenue. Meg, too distracted by her grow-ing bag of candy, started out into the road, and Mason had to put a hand in front of her.

"You gotta look." He used the same bothered tone he al-ways used with his sister. She rolled her eyes, and he added, "I gotta keep you safe, Meg."

"Fine," she said, mimicking his annoyed voice.

From across the street, a group of teens walked their way, laughing and roughhousing. As they passed, the tallest boy, who was wearing a werewolf mask, leaned into Meg's face and growled. The teens all laughed and kept walking, but Meg's hand shot into Mason's.

"It's all right," he said. "Just some dumb kids."

They walked like that up until the next house, and when Meg returned, Mason expected her to reach for his hand once more. She never did.

CHAPTER 5

The Scarecrow

Meg didn't quite understand what was happening between her and Mason, but she knew her brother was changing, turning into someone she didn't like very much. It didn't matter who started it, once they started bickering, there was no stopping it. It was so constant that it seemed as if they didn't even like each other, not the way they used to. He was her big brother, and it was Halloween, and that used to mean something special.

The bitter energy grew and swelled up inside her as they went from house to house, and soon she realized she was barely even acknowledging her brother anymore. It was easier to just focus on the candy. Serge was his usual friendly self, smiling and teasing her, which only made Mason seem worse by comparison.

Whatever happens to teenagers, she thought, *please don't let it happen to me.*

They had crossed over Orville and were beginning to

make their way back when Meg heard the girl scream Serge's name from across the street. She glanced up and saw two girls coming their way. One was a bubbly zombie in a cheerleader outfit. Her hair was pulled up into two wild pigtails that looked like dandelion puffs. The other, a dark-haired girl, was wearing blue hospital scrubs. There were a few dabs of red on the front of her top, but other than that, she looked like she was just getting off work.

"Come on." Meg tugged Mason's arm in the opposite direction as the two girls hurried toward them.

"Hang on," Mason said. "This will only take a second."

They'd almost made it to the west end of Orville Avenue. Just a few more houses and the road would end in a cul-de-sac where the old woods stretched beyond, a land of giant, ancient trees and rolling hills. It felt like the end of the world to Meg, and in a lot of ways it was. She could ride her bike up and down the sidewalks of Orville Avenue, but the woods were strictly off-limits.

"Hey, Serge." The cheerleader girl was clearly in love with her brother's best friend, but as far as Meg could tell, the other one didn't have much interest in Mason at all. Just then, an older woman with frizzy blond hair came running up to them. She was wearing a fancy red dress and pale makeup with fake blood dripping from the corners of her mouth.

"Mari!" the woman cried as she approached, clicking along on her high heels. The dark-haired girl turned to her friend, her eyes growing wide with embarrassment.

"Hang on a sec," she said, then spun around. "Mom, what is it?"

"I didn't give you the address to the party," the woman said, fumbling in her small purse. "I'll probably be out half the night, and I know how you kids like to wander, so if you need me, you can just stop by. It should be right here . . . oh, dang it, I left it at home."

"Mom, seriously, I'll be fine. I'll probably be home before you are."

Meg was surprised to see tears forming in the woman's eyes as she shook her head in frustration.

"Mari, I just want you to have a good time, and I'm worried you're not going to enjoy Halloween. You don't even have a costume or anything—"

"Look," Mari said, cutting her mom off and slinging an arm over the cheerleader's shoulders. "We're having fun, see? Trust me."

That seemed to appease her mother just enough to make a smile bloom on her face.

"You better," she said as she kissed Mari on the cheek. She turned and flashed a smile at the cheerleader. "Bye, Becca—you girls enjoy yourselves!" With a wave, she clicked away into the night. Mari finally turned back around and smiled at the rest of the group.

"Sorry about that."

"No worries," Serge said. "Y'all know my boy Mason, right?"

"Uh, sure," Becca said. "And you guys know Mari, don't you?"

Mason nodded. Meg couldn't remember if she had ever seen her brother look more annoyed.

"Yeah. We were in science last year."

"That's right," Mari replied. "Nice costume. Ash, right?"

"Yeah. Not the Pokémon one."

"And zombie cheerleader?" Serge asked.

"Yep," Becca said, beaming.

"And . . ." Serge said, pointing at Mari, struggling to figure out what she was dressed as.

"I'm a . . . killer nurse," she muttered. "I wasn't going to dress up, but my mom started crying, so I grabbed some of her scrubs and some food coloring. I think that at least made her a little happy. She's, uh . . . well, you saw. She's kind of a handful."

An awkward silence fell over the group, and Meg decided she had seen enough of the teenage world.

"I'm going to that house," she told Mason, pointing.

He sighed. "This is Meg. My sister. I . . . take her out trick-or-treating."

"That's nice of you," Mari said.

"Yeah," Mason said with another sigh.

Mason gave Meg a look that she was very familiar with. It was a look that said, *Please wrap this up . . . I have better things to do.* Meanwhile, Serge and Becca were laughing and chatting without a care in the world.

"Okay then," Meg said. "I'm going now."

She walked down the sidewalk, running one hand along a picket fence, relieved to leave the teens behind. Meg was focused. On Halloween, you had to be. It was a mission, and the objective was to *get the candy*. Mason used to understand that. Years before, back when he wasn't too cool for her, they'd attack the street with perfect precision, never missing a single house. They would each come home with a haul big enough to last them until Valentine's Day. Those were good days. When Mason would actually play with the toys he had arranged all over his desk. He might have been too old, even back then, but Meg didn't care. It was fun for Godzilla to come in and wreck her Barbie Dreamhouse. She might scream, but she loved it.

Meg sighed and moved on, not ready to give up on Halloween just yet. She marched with grim determination toward the next house up the block when she heard an odd fluttering sound, like a bedsheet caught in the wind. She glanced up and saw a girl about her age standing in the white pool of light under a streetlight.

The girl was dressed in darkness: a black hoodie and skirt, short black hair. To Meg, she seemed to be made of shadows, which made her bone-white face all the brighter in the glow of the streetlight. Meg walked by and caught a glimpse of the girl's eyes, which were a pale, luminous blue and so striking that Meg had to look away. Meg noticed the girl was holding a doll dressed in a sky-blue princess dress that matched her own.

"She looks like you," the girl whispered, but Meg didn't slow down. She kept her eyes forward and marched, putting distance between herself and the streetlight. The girl spoke once more, and this time it sounded as if the words were whispered directly into Meg's ear.

"Stay close to your brother."

Meg yelped and spun around, but to her surprise, the sidewalk behind her was empty.

"Candy," she whispered after a deep breath, shaking off her unease. "I'm here . . . for the candy."

She continued down the street. The next yard was surrounded by a wrought-iron fence and had a handful of sparse and old-fashioned decorations. A pumpkin-headed scarecrow that glowed with a green light from within. A tangle of spiderwebs on the mailbox. A few crows resting on the porch banister. It wasn't much, but after all the over-the-top houses Meg had seen tonight, there was something pleasant about how low-key it was. She walked up the path and squinted— the house looked empty, its windows dark and lifeless. A large bowl sat on the porch with a sign that read *Take one or take a few . . . the choice is yours.*

Meg reached into the bowl and grabbed a mini candy bar, then glanced around before grabbing another. She was halfway back down the path when she heard something shuffling behind her. Meg spun around. An old woman in a red cloak with a spiderweb pattern stood on the porch. Meg struggled to recall the woman's name. She was a quiet but friendly neighbor who tended to keep to herself. She held a wooden walking stick with an odd face carved on the top.

"Th-thank you," Meg stammered.

"You're most welcome," the woman said with a gentle smile.

The woman whispered to herself, hissing words that Meg

couldn't quite make out, and the wind whipped by, flipping up the hem of her dress. She seemed to be looking past Meg, at something behind her.

The old woman nodded.

Meg suddenly felt very cold and very alone, and when she turned around, the path back to the street was blocked by a decoration that hadn't been there before—the scarecrow. It was huge, maybe nine feet tall or more, and it blotted out the streetlight, casting Meg in a vast shadow. Somehow its greenish, ghostly light was burning brighter. A pair of spindly tree branches reached out from a black overcoat that stretched all the way to the ground. Meg stared at the horrible thing for a long moment, convincing herself it was all a prank. An older kid must have moved it into her path. Older kids always did stuff like that, especially on Halloween.

Meg took a step forward. Then another.

The scarecrow *twitched*.

It wasn't much. It might have been the wind. Whatever it was, Meg knew it wasn't her imagination because she heard one of the scarecrow's branches crack. The sound made her want to scream. She could still see Mason and his friends talking, and she couldn't believe that he didn't notice her standing there, stuck like a mouse in front of a silent cat. She looked back up at the pumpkin head. A long thread of *something* was hanging from its grim, toothy, sharklike mouth. Pumpkin guts. Orange, stringy, and filled with seeds.

The scarecrow was *drooling*.

It was too much, and Meg took a step back. Something

snapped toward her, and she looked down. A brittle, bony hand had wrapped around one of her wrists, and when she looked up again, the pumpkin's face was leering down at her, grinning and hungry. The last thing Meg could do before being whisked up off the ground was to scream her brother's name.

CHAPTER 6

Remember Who?

"They're hitting it off," Mason said to Mari. They were slowly walking a few steps ahead of Becca and Serge, and from the sound of it, he had just said something *hilarious*.

"That's putting it lightly," she said.

"I'm guessing Becca likes the jock types," Mason said.

"She's a bigger nerd than you might think," Mari said.

"Oh, I'm sure," Mason said dismissively.

"For real," Mari said. "She got hooked on gem collecting in fourth grade. Half her room was geodes and rock tumblers."

Mason burst out laughing. "Hey, everyone's into something, I guess."

"Okay, so I'll admit I looked up Ash Williams," Mari said.

Mason couldn't believe it. She'd *actually* looked something up because of him. The odds of such a thing happening were so monumentally inconceivable that it wasn't even worth doing the math. The fact that Mari now knew about the coolest horror movie hero ever was just icing on the cake.

"It's a pretty good costume," she added, "but doesn't Ash have like a chain saw for a hand?"

"Well, technically, his hand gets possessed and he cuts it off and *then* he attaches a chain saw to his arm. I tried to convince my dad to let me take his, but no, no, no, that's too dangerous."

"I mean, he's probably got a point," Mari said.

"What does that mean?"

"You're just a little . . . how can I say it? High-strung? I wouldn't want you operating any heavy equipment around me, let's put it that way."

"You know, my mom says that all the time, but let me tell you why you're both wrong—"

"MA*SONNNN*!"

Mason turned his head so fast that it made him dizzy. Meg's voice wasn't far away. After all, she had just been in sight. Sure, he might not have been watching, but what could happen when she was *right there*? Without thinking, he ran toward the sound of her voice, trying to remember which house she said she was going to while fully aware that the girls might think he was an overprotective weirdo.

That didn't matter.

He could handle embarrassment. At this point in his life, he was an expert on the subject. What he couldn't do, what was utterly unimaginable, was losing his little sister, especially when he was the only person who had any idea of what was happening in their town. The only person who knew better.

You had one job, he thought. *One simple job, and somehow you screwed it up.*

"Meg!" he yelled as he reached the next house on the street and peered over its wrought-iron fence. She *had* to be there. He'd heard her scream just a moment earlier. Panic rose inside him, bubbling up like black seawater. If Meg had been in the yard, he would have seen her. There was nowhere to hide, other than a few decorations scattered across the grass.

"Where are you?" Mason asked, his voice beginning to shake.

A chill breeze came through the bars of the fence, and he noticed an old lady standing at the edge of the porch, gazing at the trick-or-treaters.

She looked vaguely familiar, like most of the people they had passed on Orville, but her name danced at the corners of his mind, never quite coming into focus. Suddenly, the gate was flung open and something huge barreled out into the street. The shape was a blur, but it looked like someone in a giant, strange costume, heading straight for the cul-de-sac at the end of Orville Avenue. A scarecrow maybe?

Mason froze, unsure what to do next until he heard a muffled voice.

"Mason!"

It was Meg, only her scream now came from the direction of the stranger who had left the woman's yard. *It's him,* Mason thought, though he didn't exactly know who *he* was. Either way, he felt certain that this giant mousetrap of a town had closed once again, only this time, it had caught someone very close to him.

"Meg . . ."

"Hey, what's going on?" Serge asked from just behind him.

"Meg," he said, pointing at the dark shape dashing away from them. "Someone's got her!"

Mari's eyes went wide, Becca slapped a hand to her mouth, and Serge looked over Mason's shoulders, eyes blazing.

"Come on!" Serge said with zero hesitation. "Let's go get her!"

The stranger was fleeing straight down the sidewalk, toward the end of the cul-de-sac, and Mason could catch glimpses of them as they passed in and out of the pools of light from the streetlamps. The costume was enormous, easily as large as the huge characters he saw at theme parks on family trips, only this one was moving like an Olympic sprinter. After just a few seconds of chasing, Serge quickly took the lead, and he looked back at Mason, doubt in his eyes.

"Don't wait for me," Mason yelled. "Get him!"

That was all the instruction Serge needed. He took off like a bullet, leaving the three others behind. There was a single streetlight at the end of the cul-de-sac, and Serge caught up just before the culprit made it to the woods that loomed beyond like a shadowy curtain.

"Hey, you gotta stop!" Serge yelled as he ran in front of the stranger, cutting off their path and holding up his bat like a chivalrous knight. Mason sprinted forward, and a moment later, saw the look of utter terror on his friend's face. Something was wrong. An impossibly long arm reached down and swung, swatting Serge and the bat aside.

"Stop!" Mason yelled.

The spindly frame turned. Mason heard a creaking sound, like dry branches snapping and popping, and then he finally saw what had abducted his sister.

"What. In. The. *Crap.*"

The words fell out of his mouth when he saw the glowing jack-o'-lantern head, the flaming eyes, the sharp teeth. A high-pitched scream pierced the air, and for a moment he thought, *That must be Becca.* A few seconds later, he realized it was his own voice. The scarecrow reached for him with a hand as broad as a basketball, and Mason stumbled back, falling and scrambling to get away. In that sudden rush, the black coat brushed open, and his sister's face stared back at him. She was locked inside that creature's hollowed-out tree-root body, encased in the ribs that had closed around her like the bars of a cage.

"Mason!" Meg cried, reaching between the roots. Mason gazed at her hand for a split second. Was it always so small? He knew he should reach for it, knew he should try to save her, but his body refused to listen to his brain. The sight of his sister, trapped like a tiny bird in a lion's mouth, was far too awful for him to do anything but stand there. The pumpkin head sneered before whipping the coat closed and stomping off into the woods, leaving Mason speechless at the edge of the trees.

"What was that?" Mari cried. "What the heck was that?"

Becca *was* screaming now, and she ran over to Serge, who stared at the woods as if he expected every single tree to come to life at any second. Mason was only dimly aware that Mari had come to stand beside him as he gazed into the blackness of the forest, his eyes watering. Then, without warning, he ran straight into the mouth of the woods, following the monstrous scarecrow.

Mason thought he had experienced terror before that moment. Every nightmare, every scary story, every sleepless night as his imagination ran wild from a steady diet of horror movies. It was all practice for the utter blackness of the woods. There was no path, no clear direction, nothing but the dark, shadowy spaces between the looming trees that reached down at him with gnarled fingers. All he had to go on was the vague green glow of the creature darting between the trees up ahead that had his sister.

It was fast. On concrete, Mason might have been able to keep pace, barely, but in the woods, the very thing the monster was made of, there was no chance. No matter how hard he pumped his legs, he could only watch in horror as the shape slipped farther away from him. Half a minute later, he tripped, doubled over, and fell flat on his face. When he glanced up, the green glow was gone.

"Meg!"

Mason scrambled back up and pushed forward. If the others were following, he couldn't hear them. As far as he knew, he was the only person left on the planet. Still, he stumbled forward desperately into the dark. The trees opened up, and he reached the two-lane highway that curved down into town. There were no cars in sight. He passed the familiar sign.

WELCOME TO PEARL, NORTH CAROLINA'S BEST-KEPT SECRET

Mason had never gone this far before. He, along with every other kid who lived on Orville, knew the rule: never cross the highway. The other side of that strip of asphalt was the domain of only the most bold and dangerous kids, and for the first time in his life, Mason crossed over without a second thought. The woods were just as thick on the other side, but in that darkness, he saw the green glow once more. It was closer than he realized, and he broke into a full sprint, careening toward it. A moment later, the woods thinned out to a small clearing, with the green glow shining at the center.

"Meg!"

Just as Mason entered the clearing, the green light blinked out like a candle in a breeze. He fumbled for his phone and turned on the flashlight, desperate for some sign of where the light had gone. The clearing was empty now, except for a withered husk of a giant dead tree at its center. The trail had gone cold, and there seemed to be nothing left in the woods but utter darkness and silence.

Mason trudged back the way he'd come and found the others waiting on the opposite side of the highway. All of them looked terrified and shaken by what they'd seen. Mason's entire body ached from the running and falling, but it didn't matter. They needed help.

"Come on," he said as he ran past them. "I gotta tell Mom and Dad."

Mason's sides were starting to cramp. He hadn't run this far in . . . well, maybe ever, and it was taking a toll on him. Serge was right next to him, and together they dodged through the crowds, the girls keeping pace behind them. Mason wasn't surprised that Serge was barely breathing hard. A max-effort sprint for Mason was a light jog for him.

There were hundreds of people moving up and down the street. Each time they hit a blockade of bodies on the sidewalk, they'd cut into the street and dodge around cars. They looked like guilty kids who were up to no good, but it didn't matter. Nothing mattered other than finding Meg.

"Hey!" an adult voice called out. "Where's the fire?"

Mason stopped and felt a sudden rush of hope. A cop stood at the edge of a wild party that filled several yards. To Mason's surprise, he was holding a red cup.

"I . . . I . . ."

Mason couldn't breathe. It had been years since he had had an actual asthma attack, but he could remember the familiar clenching feeling in his lungs as they refused to fill up.

"Well?" the cop asked, taking a long drink. "You need something or what, kid?"

Suddenly, Mari stepped in front of Mason. "Officer, we need your help."

The cop slowly looked from one kid to the other, then smiled broadly.

"All right, we got a little nurse . . . a zombie cheerleader . . . a baseball player . . . and whatever you are."

He took another drink, and Mason's stomach sank.

He's not going to help, he thought.

"What can I do for you, little nurse?"

"Please, we need help. His little sister was—"

"Just calm down," the cop said, putting a hand on his belt. Mason noticed the gun, the handcuffs, the pepper spray—all very official-looking and a little scary.

"Please, this is *serious,*" Becca said.

"This party is serious," he corrected her with a laugh. "Everyone, just calm down. Nothing bad happens on Halloween. Not in Pearl."

Mari stomped her foot. "A little girl has been kidnapped!" she yelled over the booming music. "Do you want that on the news tomorrow morning?"

The cop's face tightened and he hiked up his belt. "That's a big accusation, little nurse. You got any proof?"

"*Proof?*" Mari yelled. "Do I need proof to make you do your job?"

"Take it easy—"

"I need you to come with me *now,*" she said. "We need to find her before the . . . guy gets away. We need roadblocks and helicopters! Do you hear anything I'm saying?"

The cop had closed his eyes and was swaying slowly to a reggae song that had come over the closest speaker.

"I love this song," he said to himself.

"What's wrong with you?" Mason yelled when he finally caught his breath.

The cop's eyes snapped open, and he sighed heavily, clearly annoyed. "Okay," he said, "here's the deal. There's a *lot* of kids in this town, and on Halloween they play a *lot* of pranks. But it's all in good fun, you understand? Now, this kid . . . what's her name?"

"Meg!" Mason yelled.

"Well, I'm sure Meg's having a little fun with you. She's probably hiding in a bush watching you right now. I promise, it's all good, but *if it's not,* you just come find me in the morning."

He took another sip from his cup and smiled.

"But not too early, little nurse!" he added with a wag of his finger.

He turned back to the party. In the span of a second, it was as if the four of them weren't standing there. Mason felt like screaming, but he didn't have the energy to even do that. More than at any point in his entire life, he felt nothing but pure dread.

"What is wrong with this town?" Mari asked.

"I don't know," Mason said, "but we need help."

"Come on, man," Serge said, putting a hand on his shoulder. "Let's go see our parents. They'll know what to do."

Mason felt a fresh hitch in his throat as Serge pulled him along. He couldn't feel his legs moving, but somehow he was running again. Meg was gone. *Really* gone. He had to believe they'd get her back, but he was also selfishly terrified of what their parents would say.

You knew better, he thought. *Out of everyone in town, you knew.*

It couldn't be helped. The blaming would come later, after the smoke cleared, after they had Meg back. Even so, there was no denying that Mason had never been more disappointed in himself then he was now.

"I'll do the talking," Mason said, steeling himself.

Serge's house came into view, and Mason saw his own parents standing on the front porch, both dressed like the cheapest cowboys possible. The hats, tiny guns on their belts, and little plastic sheriff stars probably cost five bucks combined. They looked remarkably silly, but his eyes filled with tears when he saw them. Mason knew he was close to breaking, and he didn't want to do it in front of the girls. As though reading his mind, Serge seemed to sense what was coming.

"Maybe you two should wait here," Serge told the girls, gesturing to the sidewalk.

"Mason, what in the world are you two up to?" his mother asked as he and Serge walked up to the porch.

"I'm sorry," he said, crying and fighting to catch his breath.. "I tried to keep up with her . . . I'm so sorry. . . ."

"Serge!" Serge's dad yelled from just inside the open front door. "You better get in here and eat some of these hot dogs!"

Mason saw Serge was on the verge of tears as well, but he stayed silent, waiting for Mason to spill the horrible news.

"Just calm down there, pardner," Mason's dad said, wrapping a heavy arm around his shoulders. "What's going on, bud? Some bullies messing with you? You need ol' Sheriff Dad to deal with them?"

Mason stood up straight and sucked in a deep breath.

"It's Meg!" he said. "We were talking, and she was at the next house, just right there, not far away at all, and some . . .

thing grabbed her and carried her into the woods. I chased her, I *promise I did,* but they're gone. We gotta get back out there and look, and call the cops, and . . . and—"

"Whoa, buddy," said Mason's dad, patting his son on the back. "Just calm down, it'll be fine."

Mason's mother put a hand to his cheek. "You can't get so worked up about stuff like this, honey. What is this, a horror movie you and Serge came up with? Where's the camera?"

"Mom, there's no camera. This is *real.*"

She flipped one hand dismissively and rolled her eyes.

"I'm glad you have a good imagination," she said. "You're a pretty good actor too."

"Mom, Meg is gone!"

She looked at her husband, and they both smiled.

"Who?" she asked.

"Is that a girl from class?" his dad asked, poking him in the ribs.

Mason looked from one parent to the other, then over at Serge. His biggest fear was happening to his own family.

"Serge," she said, ignoring the panic on the boys' faces, "we got a lot of food to eat."

"Mom," Mason yelled, "you're not listening! We're looking for Meg! She's missing. Someone took her."

His mom shook her head. "Honey . . . who is *Meg?*"

Mason and Serge looked at each other, and Mason saw his own disbelief and dread reflected in his friend's face.

"She's your daughter," Mason said softly. "She's my sister."

"I think I'd remember having two kids," his mom said as

she turned to walk inside. "Get back to whatever game you're playing. It's *Halloween.* Have a good time, boys."

His dad finished a beer and shook his head. "Making up sisters." He laughed. "I gotta say . . . that's a weird one. Even for you."

"Dad," Mason said, grabbing him by his wrist, "are you really saying you don't remember her?"

He grinned. "Remember who?"

Mason's parents walked back inside to join Serge's mom and dad in laughing, eating, and drinking as if Meg had never existed. His dad glanced back once and pointed one of his toy cowboy guns at his son.

"Giddyap!"

Mason walked back to the sidewalk in a daze, his head hurting, the world spinning. The wild, fun town that fully embraced Halloween felt more warped and disturbing than ever. All around him laughing people marched past with bloody faces, grotesque masks, and absurd costumes, while his sister had seemingly vanished off the face of the earth.

"What's happening?" Serge asked, half to himself.

"*This* . . . this is how it always happens," Mason said as the awful truth washed over him. "This whole town is . . . cursed or something. They just take these kids in plain sight, and no one even knows."

He turned to Serge, his whole body shaking with fear and pain.

"They don't even *remember*."

He didn't see Mari and Becca walk up, but suddenly they

were standing beside him. Mason didn't want them to be there. He barely knew them after all, and now, all of a sudden, they had front-row seats to the worst moment of his life. He considered asking them to leave, but then he thought about how they'd both spoken up to the cop, jumping into a situation that didn't really include them.

They want to help, he thought, and his heart hurt when he realized that these near strangers would care enough to do something.

"I don't get it," Mari said. "We went and talked to two more cops, and they both just laughed it off. Told us we were being silly. That nothing bad ever happens in this town. What about you?"

Mason looked at Serge and shook his head. He couldn't even say it out loud.

"You tell them."

The news that parents had totally forgotten a child wasn't easy to hear.

"I don't believe it," Mari said, eyes wide. "It's . . . just not possible."

Becca was nervously twirling her fingers through her hair, making it even wilder than it had been before.

"Parents don't do that," Becca said. "They just *don't* forget about kids."

"They do in Pearl," Mason said, standing up straight.

"What does that mean?" Mari asked.

"Serge, can you run in and grab some flashlights?"

His friend looked uneasy, but he didn't hesitate. Mason

stared at the ground while he was gone, and the girls left him alone with his thoughts.

I lost her, he thought over and over again, in a sickening, never-ending loop.

Serge reappeared a few moments later and handed him a flashlight.

"What's the plan?" he asked.

Mason looked up, took a deep breath, and began to walk in the direction they had come from. Serge, Mari, and Becca followed him.

"I don't expect any of you to come along with me if you don't want to," Mason said. "But I have to go get her. I have to try. Meg is out there, and I know she's scared to death. Heck, *I'm* scared to death."

"Shouldn't we try to get some help?" Becca asked.

"There is no help," Mason replied. "I wish I could say there was a plan. That some grown-ups would take over. But I can't say any of that. It's us. Just *us.*"

"You saw that thing," Becca said. "It was a *monster!*"

"There's something wrong with this town," Mason said softly, with all of the certainty he'd felt for years. "It's got my sister, and I've got to get her back."

Serge put a hand on his shoulder.

"You're not doing it without me," he said. "I don't know what that thing was, but next time, I'll swing first and ask questions second."

Mari and Becca looked at each other.

"We're all in over our heads," Mari said. "But I think you

already know that. I'm not sure what I can do, but I'll at least help you look."

Everyone looked at Becca, who scrunched up her face.

"Guys," she said through gritted teeth. "A *monster.*"

"You don't have to go," Serge told her. "I won't think any less of you if you don't."

"No," she said suddenly, standing straighter. "I'll come too."

"All right," Mason said, steeling himself for whatever vast unknown awaited them. "Let's go."

CHAPTER 7

Within the Woods

The world had gone dark, and for the longest time, Meg wondered if maybe she was dead. Perhaps that's what death was, a small, tight spot with no light peeking in, a constant bumping and jumping as you were jostled around like a piece of gravel in someone's shoe. She tried to remember what had happened, tried to piece it together so she could make sense of it all.

The pumpkin-headed monster had grabbed her and tossed her into its hollowed-out chest. Like magic, the ribs had closed shut around her, and there she had stayed. There were tiny gaps here and there, and she had watched the street fly past as they headed toward the forest. There were screams, both from her and from Mason, and once she had managed to poke her arm through one of the spaces between the monster's ribs to reach for her brother. The opening was too small, and the skin of her arm was scraped painfully, and it was all for nothing. The creature easily fought her brother and his friends off and escaped into the woods.

Then it was dark, and it stayed dark for a very long while—until suddenly the footsteps stopped. In the blackness, Meg could barely make out a large shape in front of her—a tree maybe?—and then there was more blackness. What happened next was so bizarre, so hard to comprehend, that it made Meg's head spin. The monster leaned forward at an odd angle, then seemed to flip and fall. The world turned upside down, and even in the darkness, Meg could feel that her feet were somehow above her head. It was like being on a roller coaster, but worse, the feeling compressed and heavy, like gravity had doubled, tripled. She tried to scream, but she was falling too fast for the sound to escape.

Then, the world was upright once more.

"I assume the work went well, Mr. Crow?"

It was a woman's voice. There was a sudden spark of light, and Meg peered through the gaps in her makeshift cage. The woman's soft, wrinkled face was close, peering in with a smile that Meg recognized—it was her, the neighbor who had been watching her from the porch . . . her name elusive even as it appeared in Meg's mind like a dark secret.

"Ms. Vernon," she whispered, and the old woman laughed. "Spit her out."

Meg couldn't begin to understand what the old lady was doing there, or how she had made it into the woods so quickly. The scarecrow's rootlike ribs opened with a creak, and Meg fell out onto the ground like a heap of clothes. When she looked up, Ms. Vernon was standing above her, clutching a cane topped with a smiling face and eyes that glowed bright enough to illuminate the woods surrounding their little group.

"Up now," she ordered. "We don't want to keep our friends waiting. They are positively *famished*."

With that, the grotesque little face atop the cane came to life and began to laugh in a wordless wheeze. Ms. Vernon patted its head with her free hand. Meg didn't move. She was utterly frozen in fear.

"It's easier when they decide to walk," Ms. Vernon said with a sigh. "But . . . I know how stubborn children can be. My own boy was hardheaded. He learned, though. I have plenty of ways to *encourage* naughty children."

She whispered an unintelligible word, and the large spiders in her hair jerked to life and scuttled down her face, over her lips, and down her outstretched arm. She held them out to Meg as if offering her a treat. Meg leapt to her feet and backed away, only to run into Mr. Crow. She looked up, and when he smiled down at her a dribble of pumpkin guts landed on her shoulder.

"I'll walk," she said softly.

"Thought so," Ms. Vernon said. She twisted her head, and Meg heard her neck pop and crackle. It sounded like a handful of dead leaves.

"Enough of this," Ms. Vernon said, exasperated. "I've worn this *costume* long enough."

She lifted both hands to her chin and then slowly raised them up her face. And as she did, everything about her changed. As though she were wiping off heavy makeup, the real Ms. Vernon emerged. Her face was white, a perfect match for her hair, which had straightened and now draped down her shoulders in icy waterfalls. The spiders skittered this way and that to hide in the drifts of her hair. The paleness of her skin made her eyes all the more unsettling. Her irises had gone a deep, seeping red, as if she might weep blood at any moment, and her lips matched the crimson color of her eyes.

She's a witch, Meg realized. It was the sort of thing she read about in books. Witches ate children, and this was, without question, a witch. Meg could only shiver, wondering what might happen next.

Ms. Vernon's face was the most drastic part of her transformation, but her slumped frame had straightened as well. She was taller now, maybe even taller than Meg's father, who was over six feet. The wrinkles on her face had smoothed a bit, and though she still looked older, there was nothing even slightly feeble about her. She was, in a deeply terrifying way, as beautiful as she was unsettling. More so than any of Meg's teachers, more than her parents, the witch towered over Meg like a pale, monolithic statue.

Witch.

Yes. There was no doubt about it. No green skin, no warts, no pointed hat. Just that awful, otherworldly beauty.

Mr. Crow let out a garbled sound that might have been words in another language, and Ms. Vernon looked at him.

"Children?" she asked, and he nodded.

70

"Hmm . . . very well. Watch the woods. Kill them if you must."

The scarecrow tilted his head toward the ground, and he began to twist his huge hands together like a toddler caught with a cookie before dinnertime. To Meg's amazement, he seemed nervous.

"Is that . . . hesitation I sense?" Ms. Vernon asked. "Not too keen on killing them?"

The pumpkin head dipped lower. For Meg, there was no doubt.

He doesn't want to do it.

"What is this world coming to?" the witch asked. "Fine, I'll make it simple for you. Don't like your job? Then I'll find someone else, understand? And you'll go back to being a pumpkin."

Mr. Crow nodded silently, and Meg saw the resignation in his spindly shoulders.

"Good. We understand each other. Don't let anyone get past. We have our largest crowd yet this year. . . ."

She placed a hand on Meg's shoulder.

"I don't want to disappoint our guests."

The little face on her cane laughed, and Ms. Vernon stood for a moment, watching the scarecrow walk away into the forest. When he was gone, she glanced back at Meg.

"Do you know who might have followed you?"

Meg swallowed so loudly she was certain the witch heard it.

"I thought so. Family, I assume? A sister . . ." Ms. Vernon paused, studying Meg like a spider studying a fly. "Or maybe a brother?"

71

Tears prickled the corners of Meg's eyes. She knew it was bad to tell strangers anything, but this *was a witch*. She could surely get what she wanted from Meg, and there was nothing Meg could do about it.

"I suppose you think he'll come to save you, hmm?" Ms. Vernon continued. "Maybe come swooping in like a super-hero? Well, he might *try*. These darn spells . . . The bigger they get, the more complicated they are. The parents forget immediately, but you kids take more time. Something to do with your minds. The way you see the world, not all black-and-white. You're harder to bend. Ah well. It doesn't matter. There is *always* a way to deal with unwanted guests."

The witch raised her left arm. Meg wasn't sure if the bird flew down from the black sky or if she had somehow made it bloom out of thin air. Either way, a large black crow was sud-denly perched on Ms. Vernon's forearm. The witch smiled at the bird, which twisted its head and cawed loudly.

"We have guests," Ms. Vernon whispered as she held out a single finger, pointing at the crow. "I'll give you my eyes, little one."

The tip of her sharp fingernail lightly touched the crow's head, and the black bird began to change. It looked as if an invisible bucket filled with white paint was being dumped onto its head. Its black feathers changed to white, and its beak and claws soon followed. The last thing to change were its tiny black eyes, which morphed from smooth, glassy dark buttons into blood-red pits.

Ms. Vernon turned her head, and the crow mimicked her perfectly.

"Go and watch," she whispered, "and keep an eye on the scarecrow." The crow cawed and took flight. A few white feathers fluttered down, and Meg dodged them. The witch looked down at her and smiled without a hint of warmth or mercy.

CHAPTER 8

Welcome to UnderPearl

It wasn't until they were in the woods once again, wrapped in black shadows that their weak flashlights could barely push back, that Mason felt the change. He was handling this situation the same way he handled almost everything, with a manic energy that probably looked as if he were hyper-focused. He always talked a lot about plans, the words spilling from his mouth as though he hoped that if he just kept talking, he might accidentally say something clever. It mostly worked. His parents, his teachers, and most of the other kids at school thought Mason always had a plan.

Only one person knew the truth. But thankfully Serge was kind enough to keep it to himself.

The truth was that Mason was flailing through life just like every other kid his age, but the big difference was that he *hated* looking like he didn't know what he was doing. Mason would never be the captain of the football team, but he desperately wanted everyone to think he had it all together. Now, as they wandered into the woods, calling Meg's name, Mason realized that he didn't have any plan at all. His worst fear had come true. Now he was just a terrified kid, lost in the dark.

"All right, let's spread out," Mason said, willing confidence into his voice. "Shoulder to shoulder, I guess. Eyes forward."

They walked for a bit, but the dark, eerily quiet woods seemed to drain them of their energy. Time was the most important thing, and after about five minutes of aimless walking, Mason felt certain that time was getting away and taking Meg right along with it.

"Maybe we should go back to where you saw them last," Serge said. Mason could sense something familiar in his voice, a bit of encouragement that his friend always seemed willing to share when Mason was frustrated.

"Yes. That's, uhhh . . . yes."

The girls started to walk ahead of them, and Serge grabbed Mason by the shirt and whispered in his ear.

"Let me take point on this one."

He spoke with the terminology of their time spent in the world of online gaming, the domain of space marines and capture the flag. In that world, Mason was a titan, and he always knew what to do. In this world—the real world—Mason flinched at the suggestion, but Serge patted his shoulder.

"I got this," he whispered. "We're gonna get her. Trust me. I'll take the front. You watch my six."

Mason nodded, realizing this was exactly what he needed. His nerves were fried, and he needed his buddy to back him up.

"Yeah," Mason said. "Big guns up front. Covering fire in the back."

His lip was quivering, and he knew he was on the verge of tears again.

"Hey," Serge said softly, shooting him a concerned look as they began to walk again. "You never answered the question earlier . . . Saitama versus Superman."

"What?" Mason asked.

"Who would win?"

Mason smiled and wiped his nose.

"Well," he said cautiously, "too many variables—we just don't know enough to make a fair call on that one."

"You come up with an answer and let me know," Serge said with a smile as he jogged past the girls to the front of the line. "Let's pick up the pace," he said, raising his voice. "Get across the highway, to the last place Mason saw them. Maybe we can find some clues or tracks or something."

They cut across the highway, past the *Welcome to Pearl* sign, and a few minutes later, they returned to the small grove.

"Here," Mason said as they walked into the clearing. "This is where I saw them, right before they disappeared."

"All right," said Serge, "let's fan out and look around."

The grove was only about thirty feet across, and its only real feature was the giant dead tree in the center. Mason shined a light on it. Once, it must have been a towering behemoth with branches stretching far into the sky. Time had taken a toll on it, though, and most of its limbs had died and fallen off to rot. All that remained was a broad, split trunk that had gone black in the middle. As the others checked around the grove, Mason stepped forward for a closer look.

The split in the trunk was wide enough for him to step into if he had wanted, but the bottom of the hollow it created caught his eye. He leaned forward and saw the sunken hole was filled with an elaborate tangle of spiderwebs. In the center of the webs sat a massive, colorful garden spider.

That's a big one, he thought as he began to lean back. Only . . . he couldn't lean back.

It was hard to understand just what he was feeling. The closest comparison he could think of was when he was forced to hang on the pull-up bar in gym class, fighting gravity in a battle he could never win. He pushed his hands against the sides of the trunk and tried to break free, but in a rising panic, he realized he couldn't.

"Guys," he said. "I—"

The feeling of being pulled down toward the spiderwebs grew, and he screamed.

"Are you stuck?" Serge asked.

Mason couldn't turn, but he felt Serge's hand on his shoulder.

"It's pulling me down!"

More hands appeared, grabbing his shirt and his arms, and Mason realized that all three of them were pulling him back, stretching him like a piece of taffy. Every ounce of his strength was focused on breaking free from the invisible force, but it was useless. He was going down, into the blackness, to the place where only spiders lived.

"I . . . can't . . . hold it. . . ."

And as he began to slip down, he could feel that the others were caught as well. The hands that had been pulling him back released their hold, but they were still there, still pressed against him, still caught like a spaceship in a black hole. The last thing he heard was someone screaming in a high-pitched, terrified voice.

"What's going *onnnn* . . . ?"

They all went in.

The world tumbled, turned, changing into sickening, spinning blackness. Up was down, down was left, feet were heads. Somewhere in that chaos, Mason heard his friends screaming, but their screams were distant, like coins thrown into an empty well. Then, as quickly as it started, the iron grip of gravity let them go, and they landed in a heap on the ground. Serge's foot was on the side of Mason's face, and he shook it off and stood up.

"What . . . was . . . that?" Serge asked.

Mason picked up his flashlight. It felt like they had traveled a thousand miles, but they were still in the woods, still in the shadow of the old dead tree.

"It was like being sucked out into space or something," Mari said.

"I *really* hope that doesn't happen again," Becca said.

"Look," Mason said, his voice shaking. The beam of his flashlight had fallen on a sign posted at the edge of the clearing. Scrawled in red paint, it read *Town This Way*, with an arrow pointing in the direction they'd come from.

"How the heck did we miss that?" Mari asked.

"Wait," Mason said. "Be quiet. . . ."

Silence fell over them.

"Do you hear that?" Mason asked.

"I don't hear anything," Serge answered.

"Exactly!" Mason said. "No crickets. No birds. No breeze. Just . . . nothing." His mind spun. "Turn off the flashlights," he said, and when they did, he looked up at the sky.

"Something's not right," he said. "Come on."

They ran back the way they had come, not stopping until they saw the highway again. Once the sky was clear, Mason stared up at it.

"There are no stars," he said.

"It's just cloudy," Becca replied.

"No," Mari said, fear growing in her voice. "It's something else. Something's wrong."

The sky was dark, but when Mason really stared at it, he could see that there was something . . . off about it. Directly overhead it was a patchy brown color, with bits of gray mixed in with the darkness. Hard as it was to believe, the sky seemed closer.

"I don't understand," Serge said.

"Guys . . . ," Mason whispered.

Once again, his light was trained on a spot ahead of them.

It was the huge *Welcome to Pearl* sign, only someone had changed it. The addition to the sign was scrawled in the same red as the smaller sign, but Mason was beginning to wonder if it was paint at all. The new sign read:

WELCOME TO UNDERPEARL.

CHAPTER 9

A Tangled Web

"UnderPearl," Serge read aloud. "What's that?"

"Okay," Mason said, trying not to panic. "We just need to go back into town and . . ."

"And what?" Becca yelled.

"Becca, calm down," Mari said, reaching for her arm.

"No!" Becca swatted her friend's hand away. "I'm sorry about your sister," she said, facing Mason, "I really am, but I've had enough. I . . . I need to go home."

She's cracking, Mason thought, and he cut his eyes over at Serge, who looked just as lost as he felt.

"Just take a breath," Serge said.

"No! I have to go," Becca said.

She turned toward town but froze at the sudden sound of footsteps behind them, coming from the direction of the hollow tree. The four of them shared a quick glance before dashing behind the nearest group of trees. Mason saw Becca slap a hand over her mouth to stifle a scream as they waited to see who would emerge. The shuffling steps grew closer.

"Every year," a voice growled, "it gets harder and harder to find the time to break away."

"Well, it's only one day a year," a second voice answered. "And it's totally worth it for the food alone."

The unseen strangers walked uncomfortably close to Mason's hiding spot, and he held his breath. A moment later, he heard their feet padding softly on the pavement as they passed by.

They're not wearing shoes, he thought.

Mason waited a few more moments before he dared to look at his friends. A dozen feet away, Becca was shaking her head. Serge stood next to her, and when he stuck his head out gingerly for a peek, his eyes grew wide. Mason cringed and leaned out as well.

At first, he thought it was nothing more than a couple out for Halloween. They were both dressed as mummies, complete with filthy, moldy rags that hung down and dragged on the pavement. They were good costumes, expensive from the look of it, only there was something not quite right about them. They were *too* good somehow, like costumes from a movie set.

"Serpa can be a pain, but she puts on the *best* parties," the man said, and as he spoke, he turned just enough for Mason to see his face. Half of his jaw was devoid of skin, a slice of yellowing bone visible. One eye was gone as well, but something milled around in the empty black hole.

Beetles, Mason thought with a casualness that terrified him. *Or worms maybe.*

The other half of the face was shriveled, the dry skin pressed tightly to the skull. When the man spoke, Mason could hear his teeth clatter.

"Don't let that old *witch* ruin our fun," the woman said. "We'll have a wonderful night, my love." Somehow, her face was even fouler than the man's. The thin sheet of skin on her cheek had *shifted,* sliding down it like a slice of ham thrown against a car window. Her eye socket was two inches too low, but it didn't seem to bother her. Her eyeball dangled on a thread next to her chin.

"Now, give us a kiss," she said, and as they pressed their lipless grins together, a snake slithered out of her mouth and into the man's. It never came back out, and Mason realized it must have curled down his throat and into his stomach.

Maybe it's taking a nap, Mason thought wildly.

The happy couple locked decrepit hands and shuffled off toward the town. Once they were completely out of sight, the four friends emerged from their hiding places. Mason stared down at the ground, and a single word echoed in his mind over and over.

Monsters . . .

"Okay, I think we need to—" Mason said, but Becca promptly cut him off.

"Monster," she said. Not a question, just a simple, plain fact.

Mari stood next to her, placing a gentle hand on Becca's

shoulder, but it didn't matter. Mason saw it, the way Becca shook her head, the way her eyes looked wilder, like those of a coyote in headlights. The fear had broken something inside her, and she was silently, totally losing it.

"Just breathe," Serge said.

"Did you see it?" she asked. "Did you see it? It's real. They're monsters. . . ."

By then, Mason was already studying the path behind them.

"It's like they're headed into town for something. I guess that's who the sign was set up for."

"They're real!" Becca screamed.

"Look, just calm down," Serge said.

"I'm calling my mom," she said, fumbling with her phone. "My phone's not working."

"Neither is mine," Mari said.

"My phone's not working," Becca repeated. "Why isn't *my phone working*?"

"Keep your voice down!" Mason said.

"No!"

Panic had taken hold of her. Mason recognized it because he'd felt it himself. It was the urge to run when you were walking in a dark place alone. It was the monster behind you, the thing just out of sight, and before you knew it, your quick walk had become a sprint as you did everything possible to put space between you and the thing at your heels. That feeling had hold of Becca and there was nothing left but pure, unequaled terror.

She ran.

Not even Serge could catch her. She had madness in her feet, like wind pushing a sailboat. The others were screaming after her, begging her to stop, but it was clear that she was beyond listening. She was on the road in a few seconds, running away from town as fast as her legs could carry her, her curls whipping in the wind.

It was a mad rush for all of them, but somehow, moments before it happened, Mason saw the danger rising up to meet them. It was still dark, even darker now thanks to the odd, lightless sky, but he could make out something looming in the road ahead of them, some new blackness that his mind couldn't quite process until they were practically on top of it. Thirty or so yards from the UnderPearl sign, the road simply ended. It didn't veer to one side or turn from asphalt to gravel. It just ceased to be.

"Watch out!" Mason yelled just a second too late. Becca disappeared over the edge and into an abyss.

Mari and Serge both screamed as she vanished, and the three of them came to a halt at the edge of the precipice. Mason held his breath as he peered carefully over, terrified of what he might see. A gauzy, vague substance hung in the air. It looked to Mason like a bank of fog, but more solid somehow. In the center of it, hanging in midair twenty feet down, was Becca.

"Becca, are you okay?" Mari cried.

"I . . . I think so."

The fall seemed to have replaced her terror with confusion.

"Where am I?" she called up.

"No clue," Serge said. "But hang on, I'll try to get down there."

Mason's brain was still fighting to process what he was seeing. It looked like a giant had picked up the entire town, ripping it out of the ground. The wall beneath them was jagged and uneven, but Serge was able to find enough footholds and started to climb down it.

"What *is* all this?" Becca asked.

"I don't know," Mari replied. "Just keep your eyes on me, okay? We'll get you . . ."

Mari's voice trailed off as she gazed out and into the distance. Mason saw it as well, a hulking shape out there in all that fog.

No, Mason thought. *It's not fog.*

"Guys, I'm stuck in something. It's sticky."

Mason's eyes were adjusting to the dark, and he finally realized what he was seeing.

"Serge," he said, trying to keep his voice calm. "You gotta hurry."

Becca yelped suddenly and her body swayed back and forth, like a hammock in a swift breeze.

"What was that?" she asked.

"What was what?" Mari replied.

"You didn't feel that? Everything's shaking. . . ."

Mason shined the light down on Becca and realized the awful truth. She had fallen into a spiderweb, a web unlike any he'd ever seen. The strands were thick braids, easily strong enough to hold something much bigger than Becca. The web was bouncing up and down, and as Mason slowly raised the flashlight, he saw why.

"Oh no . . ."

It was hard to say exactly how big the spider heading Becca's way was. Maybe as small as a dump truck. Maybe as big as a house. The simple fact was, Mason had nothing to compare it to. Spiders were small and delicate, things that mean little boys crushed under their feet. This was a monster, with legs big enough to crush eight mean little boys at once.

Big enough to make a meal out of the girl now stuck in its web.

It's a garden spider, Mason thought, and for a moment, he actually marveled at its beautiful mixture of yellow-and-black patterns. Then he remembered Mr. Burkitt's science class, and an awful thought echoed inside his head. *Spider venom liquifies the inside of insects.*

Mari had seen the spider too. Her flashlight was shaking in her hand, and her mouth hung open in a wordless scream. Serge had just made it halfway down the wall when he looked over his shoulder and saw it.

"Is that a *spider*?" he yelled.

"Is what a . . . ?" Becca asked as she tilted her head back. *"SPIDER!"*

Mason had never seen anyone move so fast. Becca never stopped screaming as she peeled herself out of the web, one arm and then the other. A few moments later, she was on her feet, clinging to the edge of the jagged wall as the web continued to bob and bounce toward her.

"Don't look back!" Mari yelled. "Just climb!"

Becca looked back. She couldn't help it, and her scream rattled Mason's bones. The spider, which had seemed so far away, was close now, so close that Mason could see its eyes shining like empty black buttons. Somehow, Serge had made it far enough down the wall to reach Becca, and he yanked her out of the tangle of webs.

"Come on, you can make it!" Mari cried.

All Mason could do was watch with the surreal feeling that he was trapped inside a nightmare. Serge pulled Becca up to a small outcropping halfway up the wall, and he quickly swapped places with her, pushing her up from underneath. Mason couldn't believe it, how instantly selfless Serge was.

There's a giant spider, he thought, *and Serge is helping her up first.*

"You have to hurry!" Mari screamed.

Becca was within arm's reach now, and Mari and Mason each took an arm. The moment she was clear, Serge bounded up behind her, and the four of them ran. Mason didn't glance back until they were once more in the woods, hidden within the safety of the trees. A pair of enormous black legs rolled over the crest of the wall followed by a giant, eight-eyed head that searched the edge of the cliff. A moment later, it receded back into the blackness to wait in patient silence.

They ran all the way back to the Welcome sign and collapsed in a heap. As the others panted and caught their breath, Mason kept his eyes and ears open to their surroundings.

Monsters, he thought as he adjusted his glasses. *The sign. The sky. The spider.*

He couldn't even begin to make sense of it all. It felt as

though a tornado had blown through his room, stirring up all the movie posters, the toys, and the horror books before slamming his TV against his head. That seemed like a more realistic scenario—that he was sitting in a hospital bed with a concussion.

"What is *happening*?" Becca said, leaning on Serge.

"It's okay," Serge said, patting her back. "It's gone now."

"You saved me," she said. "Thank you so much . . ." Her voice broke and she buried her face in his chest.

"It's . . . uh, no problem," he said, awkwardly patting her back. "You would have done the same for me."

Becca leaned back and looked at him for a long while. She seemed to be considering the idea that she might be called upon to return the favor.

"Thank you," she repeated solemnly.

"What in the world is going on here?" Mari asked.

"I . . . I don't get it," Mason replied, still scanning the horizon and looking up at the sky. "The spider," he muttered, half to himself, his mind straining to puzzle everything out.

"What about it?" Serge asked.

"It was a garden spider," he replied.

"Yeah," Serge answered. "What's that got to do with anything?"

"It was a giant spider," Mason said, again mostly to himself. "No . . . a garden spider. They're all over the bushes outside our house. They're everywhere . . . even big ones are small enough to fit in your hand."

"You're mumbling, dude," Serge said.

"Yeah . . ." Mason nodded, thinking hard. *The sign. The*

sky . . . And then everything clicked. "It's not a giant spider. It's just a *spider*."

Becca and Serge looked at each other, and Mason could see they thought he'd lost it. Only Mari seemed to follow him.

"I think I see what you're saying," she said. "It's just a regular spider, but somehow—"

"We're smaller," Mason said, finishing her thought.

"That doesn't make any sense," Becca said. "Plus, *that thing almost killed me!*"

"It was closer than you think," a new, unfamiliar voice said from behind them.

Mason spun around and shined the light toward the woods. It was hard to say exactly what he saw in those first few moments. A billowing sound surrounded him and his friends, like heavy fabric caught in the wind, and he could have sworn he saw a black cloak whipping and flailing behind a large tree. It was gone a split second later, and then he saw her. The girl was small, as small as Meg, and she was wearing a black hoodie pulled up over her head. Her cheeks were sunken, her eyes pale blue.

Skeletal.

"Who are you?" Mason asked, holding up his flashlight as though he might need to use it as a club.

"Easy, tough guy," she said with a smile. "You'll end up spraining your wrist with that thing."

The girl leaned back, stretching and yawning as if she'd just woken up from a long nap. Then she smiled at Becca. "That spider almost had your number, didn't it?"

Becca didn't answer, just stared at the girl, still shaking in terror.

"Hey," the girl continued, "it's okay. It didn't get you, but even if it did . . . it's still *okay*."

Mason was confused by everything that was happening, but the oddest thing of all was Becca's face. She was nodding. The girl smiled at the rest of them.

"So . . . quite a night, huh?"

"Who are you?" Mason asked. "Actually, it doesn't matter. My sister's missing, and we don't have time for this."

"I agree with that," she said. "You don't have much time at all. When this night is over, more than one of you might have lost someone very dear to you. And that might be the best-case scenario. Truth be told, there's no guarantee that *any* of you four will survive."

Her words hung like a thick fog over the group. From the moment that Meg had been taken, the danger had been clear to Mason, but he hadn't considered that one of them—or maybe all of them—might not make it through the night. The back of his neck prickled.

"Okay," he said. "We're listening. Now, who are you?"

"Hmm . . . now *that* is a good question."

"Look," Mason snapped, "you can't just show up all gloom and doom and not even tell us who you are."

"Ooh," the girl replied with a grin, "I like that. Call me Gloom."

"Okay . . . *Gloom*," he replied. "What exactly do you want?"

"Your blond friend had a *very* close call back there." She nodded in Becca's direction. "Brushes with death are . . . well, let's just say that's my business. But she looks fit as a fiddle now, doesn't she?"

Mason glanced over at Becca, who still looked calm even though she had started to twitch a bit.

"So, if I'm not needed here, I'll just be on my way," Gloom said, and turned to leave.

"Wait," Mason said, stopping her. "Do you actually know what's going on here?"

Gloom turned back, one eyebrow raised. "I know a lot of things, but I'm not supposed to really hang out. I've got a lot on my plate at the moment. . . ." She trailed off, distracted. Then she looked up at Mason. "I'm sure you can relate."

Mason nodded gravely. "My sister is missing."

She shot him a thoughtful look, and her face suddenly looked much older. "Yes . . . sad business all around. I wish I could help, but . . ."

"Why can't you?" Mason asked.

"Like I said, I've got my own problems. A big red magical problem."

"Maybe," Mari said, stepping forward, "we can help each other."

Gloom's eyebrows raised as she considered the idea. "I'm listening."

"Yeah," Mason said, "we can totally help. I mean, we're kind of in the dark here, so maybe if you can give us information, we can help you out too. . . ."

Gloom's eyes narrowed as she looked from one kid to the other, carefully weighing her decision.

"Fine," she said with a sudden swipe of her hand. "Just

this once, we can help each other out. But, before we can do anything else, I have to make you understand what's going on here. Words don't really do it justice. You need to see it for yourselves. Come on."

She walked past them and into the darkness, without so much as a candle to light her way. Mason glanced at Serge. If there were any monsters or giant spiders in the woods, she didn't seem too bothered by it.

"I don't think she's human," Mason whispered.

"Does it matter?" Serge asked.

Mason hesitated, then shook his head. This strange girl was their best shot at getting some answers, so they followed her silently along the path, and in a few minutes, the lights of Orville Avenue appeared once again, winking through the trees.

"Thank God," Becca said as she pushed past the others.

"Not so fast," Gloom cautioned. "It's not what you think. Go ahead and take a look, but stay out of sight."

The four of them crept past the tree line, careful to stay in the shadows, and peered out. Under the streetlights, people were walking, talking, and trick-or-treating. Everything looked normal.

"What are we looking for?" Mason whispered.

"Look again," Gloom whispered. "Look *closer.*"

Mason spied the pair of mummies among the crowd, and to his surprise, no one was panicking as they walked past. It was, as far as he could tell, just a regular gathering of Halloween fans. Until he saw the man with the red face.

It was hard to say exactly what he *was.* A pair of black

horns jutted out of his forehead, and his face was a deep blood red. Tusks jutted from the bottom of his mouth, and black drool leaked from his open maw. At a glance, Mason thought it was a devil mask of some kind, but the mouth moved, the eyes blinked, and the entire face was horribly *alive.*

A moment later, a giant eyeball appeared behind him, walking by on a black stalk that split at the bottom. It scurried around like an octopus across the seafloor. The eyeball creature bumped into the devil-faced man, and the two of them nodded like old friends and courteously moved aside for each other.

The monsters, Mason thought. *They're not costumes. They're . . . real.*

Once he saw the truth, the new world they found themselves in unfolded. It was almost too much to take in. The end of the street teemed with countless monsters. A shambling pile of seaweed wrapped in rusting chains. An empty, torn dress, dabbled with blood, draped over what must have been an invisible woman. A trio of skeletons, all holding rusted swords. A knee-high teddy bear clutching a bloody ice pick. All the way up Orville Avenue, they marched, they laughed, and, to Mason's utter amazement, they stopped at the houses to trick-or-treat.

When a man with a fish head and flopping, slimy feet approached the closest house, Mason expected to see a terrified human within, screaming and trying not to lose their mind at the sight. Instead, the door swung open and a black tentacle reached out and dropped a piece of candy into the fish man's hand.

Mason heard a muffled cry at his side and turned to see Serge holding a hand over Becca's mouth to keep her from screaming. Gloom motioned them back into the woods, and the four friends walked in stunned silence until they were back at the highway, far from the madness of the town.

"What did we just see?" Mason said.

Gloom smiled and motioned to the sky. "This . . . place. It's like a copy. This isn't Pearl." She pointed to the sign. "She calls it UnderPearl."

"Who is *she*?" Mari asked.

"The witch."

CHAPTER 10

Witches
and Spells

Mari sat down in the middle of the road. She looked dazed, like someone who had just been in a car wreck. Becca was curled up in the grass a few feet away. Serge stood on the side of the road, eyes open wide, baseball bat in hand as if he expected a monster to leap from the woods at any moment.

"Okay," Mason said, pacing back and forth. "What witch?"

"She lives in this town," Gloom said, a bit distracted as she rifled through the small bag she kept on her hip. Almost as an afterthought, she pulled out a small doll of an old, white-haired man with a big gray beard. He had a large, friendly grin on his face.

"Hmm," she said to herself. "Nashville."

"Nashville?" Mason said.

A brief look of sadness danced across her dark eyes, but it was gone in an instant.

"Sorry," she replied, stuffing the doll back into her bag as if she had been checking her phone. "Work stuff. Anyway, yes, there's been a witch living in this town for a very long time. She likes to hide in plain sight, acting like a doddering old woman, looking weak. It makes it easier to . . . do what she does."

"Who is she?" Mari asked.

"She calls herself Samantha Vernon."

"It sounds kind of familiar," Mason said, but from his friends' blank expressions, he could tell that none of them knew who Gloom was talking about.

"If you can't remember her, it's all part of her design. The spell on this place helps her blend in so she becomes almost invisible to the people who live here, especially children. You could have walked past her house a thousand times and barely remember that she lives there."

Mason shook his head, trying to picture the spot where Meg had been taken. He knew it was on the west end of Orville, but . . . wait, maybe it was near the middle of Orville?

"You're right," Mason said. "I think I saw someone when Meg was taken, but . . . I can't picture anything now."

"That's how strong her magic is. That name is just the mask she wears to hide. Her true name, the name given by the great darkness she calls master, is Serpa Vernon, or as she likes to call herself, the Red Witch of Pearl. This little game of hers is something she's been doing for years."

"You mean the kids, right?" Mason said, feeling sick as he pictured his sister's face when she reached for him through the scarecrow's ribs.

"Yes. She's been taking one a year for quite a while now. You sister is just the latest in a long line."

Mason cut his eyes over at Serge. "I knew it."

"Congratulations," Gloom said. "She works for a very specific clientele. This town, or should I say this *copy* of a town, is something she keeps hidden. She makes it once a year on Halloween, and when the night is over, she *unmakes* it. You stumbled onto it, of course, when you poked your head into that little hole. You found its entrance, and somewhere inside, there's an exit, and they're both one way only. Plus, it takes a lot of work to hide an entire town, so that's why you've all shrunk."

"Wait," Becca said, rolling over, "we're *actually* small?"

"I knew that too!" Mason said, so pleased to be proved right that he forgot his panic for a moment.

"Yep. Half an hour ago, you could have stepped on that spider and never even known it."

"And the sky?" Mari asked.

"Well, it's not really the sky at all, is it?" Gloom asked, pointing upward. "It's the inside of that old dead tree. We're all standing in a town the size of a thimble and caught in a literal spiderweb as we speak."

Mason felt suddenly sick to his stomach as he realized how precarious their situation was. He pictured a stray cat leaping into the tree and swatting the entire town into oblivion. He cast his eyes skyward. "We're *inside* the dead tree. But . . . how?"

"Well, it's what witches do best," Gloom replied, "at least, the good ones. It's a spell of course. Your witch is *very* old, and she's quite clever. She knows all manner of spells for simple things like moving objects or starting fires. But her true strength comes in her ability to *make* spells."

"I don't understand," Mason replied.

"No, I don't imagine you do. And why would you? None of you understand the ways of magic. Real magic, not phones and video games. Every spell, from the smallest spoken word to . . . well, this copy of a town, is *alive*."

Gloom emphasized the last word as if she were trying to explain the weather to a toddler.

"Okay, enough," Mason said, his head spinning. "This Hogwarts class is all very fascinating, but we need to find my sister."

"Yeah," Mari added, "why are you telling us all this?"

"At the end of the day, we want the same thing," Gloom answered. "Your sister is part of the witch's little game now. All those monsters you saw . . . she draws them here. Invites them. For a small fee, she gives them a chance to be like humans for once."

She glanced toward town, smiling almost wistfully.

"It's a bit sweet when you think about it. They may be bloodthirsty, murderous creatures, but those monsters want a night that's just for them as well. A place where they can be themselves, even just for a little while. After all, even monsters love a treat, and that's what she's giving them. But it comes at a high price. That's where your sister comes in."

"What do you mean?" Mason asked. "What do they need her for?"

Gloom's face darkened, something that didn't seem possible a moment earlier, but she still managed to smile.

"If I were you, I'd get going. Your answers are out *there*. If you hurry, you might be able to find your sister, and if so . . . all my little stories won't even matter."

With that, Gloom stood up and started walking into the woods.

"Wait," Mason said, "where are you going?"

Gloom shrugged. "I didn't get an invitation to the party, but Serpa can't keep me out."

"What are we supposed to do?" Mason asked.

"I said I'd help," she replied, not slowing down. "I didn't say I'd do everything. I'm already breaking a dozen rules by helping you at all, but if you can get rid of the witch, you'll be doing me a huge favor. As for what's next, you'll figure something out."

With that, the girl vanished into the woods. Mason watched her go, and when he looked back, he found the rest of the group standing in silence.

"Well," he said, "any ideas?"

CHAPTER 11

They're Coming for You

Standing at the edge of the lit-up, monstrous world of Under-Pearl made Mason feel like he was standing on the edge of a cliff, trying to talk himself into jumping off.

"Okay," he said. "It's a simple plan, and we have *plenty* of time." They stood shoulder to shoulder, hidden by the brush that bordered Orville, watching the monsters come and go.

"Maybe review the plan one more time," Becca said, her voice cracking slightly. Mason understood where she was coming from. She didn't want to go out there. None of them did. It was terrifying enough to just stand in the dark, watching the groups of monsters in the distance. The idea of actually walking out there was beyond all comprehension.

"First, we find Meg," Mason said. "Then we find the way out. Easy."

"No offense," Mari said, "but that's not a plan. It's more of a goal."

"What's the difference?" Mason asked.

She sighed. "A goal is something big. Broad. Like, I'd like to go to a good college and get a good job. A *plan* is all the steps it would take to actually make that happen."

"Agree to disagree," Mason said.

"No," Mari replied. "You're wrong. You don't get to disagree on things that are wrong."

Mason was quiet for five long seconds. Finally, he said, "That's your opinion."

"All right," Serge said with a pointed look, "we know the goals. What's the plan?"

Mason considered the question. When he glanced up, he realized with some horror that the rest of the group wasn't looking at him. They were looking at Mari.

"Well," she said sheepishly, "a plan needs to be something concrete. Something small and achievable. And to do that, we should start with what we know."

"We don't know anything," Mason muttered.

"Look, I'm sorry that your sister is missing," Mari snapped. "And we're all scared right now. But I'm—*we're* trying to help you. We got sucked into this mess just like you did, so cut the attitude, okay?" Mason looked over at Serge, who was looking down at his shoes.

"Okay," he said finally. "You're right. So, what do we know?"

"There's a witch named Serpa Vernon somewhere in this town," Mari said. "She lives here. Which means at least one of us has probably seen her. We might even know her."

The three nodded.

"Anyone come to mind? Anyone that doesn't like kids or seems . . . creepy?"

Serge and Mason both shrugged. Once again, Mason felt something dancing at the edge of his mind, a familiar face connected with that name, but it drifted away like smoke in the breeze.

"Okay then, what else do we know?" Mari asked.

"We know there's a butt ton of monsters out there," Mason said, pointing. "And we got one baseball bat split between four people."

"Wait, that's not a bad starting point," Mari said.

"What do you mean?" Serge asked.

"Weapons," Mari said. "Bats or shovels or . . . I don't know, I don't use weapons."

"I'm sure my parents have stuff like that in the garage," Serge said. "I mean, I know we got a rake."

"A rake?" Mason shook his head. "We gotta do better than that." His eyebrows shot up and his eyes grew wide as a possibility hit him. "Dude . . . Mr. Kirby's house."

"The vice principal?" Becca asked.

"Yes!" Mason said, triumph surging through him. "I mean, he's the creepiest dude in town, but everyone says he's got an armory in his house somewhere."

"I think that's just a rumor," Serge said.

"No way, man," Mason said. "He had a knife on him at school."

"Pretty sure he's not allowed to carry knives," Becca said.

"I know what I saw," Mason insisted. "Plus, his house

is only a few blocks away. It's the only one that's never decorated."

"It's a decent place to start at least," Serge said. "We can't just hang out here all night."

"Fine," Mari said, looking back down the street. "Let's go for the backyards on the left side. The woods go straight down Orville, so we can stay out of sight. We move quick but quiet, and most of all, we stick—"

But she didn't get the last word out of her mouth. She couldn't because she was suddenly rising up off the ground. Mason glanced back, and in the chaos that followed, he had a surprisingly calm thought.

The scarecrow is back.

The pumpkin-headed monstrosity was holding both Mari and Becca off the ground as if they were action figures. Mason's entire body locked up as his gaze met those flaming eyes and the stench of scorched pumpkin filled his nose.

Fortunately for the group, Serge wasn't one to freeze, at least not for long. A long orange blob of pumpkin guts fell onto Becca's shoulders as she squirmed. Serge's face twisted into a sneer.

"He ruined her costume," Serge hissed through his teeth as he launched himself forward, bat held overhead, swinging it like an insane lumberjack straight down between Becca and Mari. It was a stretch to reach the scarecrow's head, but Serge was able to connect, hitting him right between his evil, slitted eyes.

Mason didn't know if a baseball bat could hurt an enchanted scarecrow, but it definitely did something. The giant hands unfurled and both girls fell coughing to the ground. The sight of them gasping for air jolted Mason from the spell he was under. He reached for Mari, helping her to her feet as Serge did the same for Becca.

"Come on," Serge said as the scarecrow took a knee and rubbed his dented, orange face.

The group dashed down the tree line, toward the backyards of the closest houses. Mason wasn't surprised when Serge took the lead, sprinting toward the cover of the closest back porch. Unlike the decorated, brightly lit front yards, the backyards were dark, and Mason caught his shin on a garden gnome and went tumbling into the grass.

"Come on!" Serge snapped as he darted back and lifted Mason to his feet. Mason glanced over his shoulder and saw the scarecrow emerging from the woods with a large dent between his furious eyes.

"We need to hide," Mason said as the group began to run. "Try to give him the slip."

"We can outrun him," Serge insisted.

"Maybe you can," Mason wheezed, "but I'm toast unless we lose him."

Serge grunted but didn't argue. Instead, he pointed to the nearest house.

"Mari, Becca!" he yelled. "Try that door."

The girls were a few steps ahead, and Mari nodded, leaping up onto the small back porch and testing the door. Becca peered inside the house.

"It's empty," she said as the boys climbed onto the porch and slipped inside. Mason was the last in, and he slammed the door and leaned against it, completely spent.

"I think we lost him," he whispered.

"I don't think so," Becca said, her voice shaking. "He's going to find us, and, and . . ."

Mari put an arm around her friend and patted her back. "It's okay. Just calm down. Everyone, just try to stay calm."

They were in a small kitchen with a dining room attached. It was dark and silent, but something about the bland, simple home put Mason at ease for the first time since Meg had been taken. The door he was leaning on had a round window at its top, and he peered out gingerly.

"Do you see it?" Mari asked.

"No . . . wait!"

The glowing head came bobbing across the backyard, and Mason held his breath. The scarecrow never slowed down, and a few seconds later, it disappeared into the next yard, continuing the hunt.

"He's gone," Mason said with a deep sigh.

Relief washed over the group, and Serge immediately went and checked the surrounding rooms. When he returned a few moments later, he nodded. "I think we're safe."

"Good," Mari said. Becca was muttering softly to herself, and Mari put a hand on her shoulder to calm her down.

Mason looked at Serge. "What am I doing?" he said quietly.

Serge glanced over at the girls, then leaned closer to his friend. "Huh?"

Mason leaned against the door again, trying to steady himself. He felt like he might start screaming if he didn't say something.

"I just don't know what I'm *doing*," he said. "Meg is gone. A stupid witch has my sister, and I can't even run through a yard without tripping over a freaking garden gnome. There's no way I'm getting her back. . . ."

He trailed off, his voice getting weaker with each word.

"Knock it off," Serge said sharply. Mason looked back at him, stunned and a little hurt, but Serge didn't back down. "It's time to step up."

"What is that supposed to—"

"Stop it. Just stop. You're not perfect. Neither am I, or Mari and Becca, or anyone. No one's asking you to have a perfect plan or figure everything out. You just have to *do something*."

A bitter feeling swelled up in Mason, but before he could respond, Serge cut him off.

"Listen . . . and please don't get mad," he said in a softer tone. "Everyone else I know is like me. It's all competition, all the time. It's actually nice to have someone around who doesn't have to try to win everything, to top what I'm doing. But you can't sit it out this time. We're not going to get through the night without a fight. You want to be the hero? Well, here's your chance."

Mason glanced over at the girls and saw that they were listening in. Both of them quickly looked away.

"That's easy for the guy with the baseball bat to say," Mason said as he stood up and left the room.

Mason wasn't mad, not really, but he couldn't help himself.

Serge had a point after all. If Mason froze up every time he saw a monster, he'd never get Meg back. Even so, he couldn't let Serge know that he was right, at least not without a few minutes of sulking. So, he walked out of the kitchen, down a short hallway, and into the foyer, stopping to check around every corner. He wondered briefly whose house they were in, but there wasn't time to go searching for family photos. The place was too quiet not to be empty, but who knew what to expect in this new, monstrous world. Small windows lined the sides of the front door, and Mason peered out at the crowd that was coming and going.

There's so many of them.

The monsters were everywhere, and at this point he could only assume there were hundreds marching up and down the streets of his miniaturized hometown. As he scanned the horizon, trying to take in the full scope of the situation, a commotion on one of the side streets caught his eye. All the monsters, from the largest Sasquatch to the smallest animated porcelain dolls, were stepping aside for . . . something.

"Hey," he whispered back toward the kitchen. "Guys, come here."

Mari appeared first, and she pressed against the windows on the opposite side of the door.

"It's like a nightmare. . . ."

"Look," Mason said, pointing at the side street. "Right there. Between the two houses."

A tall man wearing overalls and a bloody pillowcase on his head glanced down, noticed something, and leapt to one side, into the street, dropping his meat cleaver as he did so.

"What are they so afraid of?" Mari asked.

By then, Becca and Serge had joined them. They were all gazing at the street when the crowd finally parted, revealing the source of the hubbub—a trio of identical monsters, all less than three feet tall, dressed in neat, matching navy-blue suits. They held hands, walking in perfect sync. Each of them had long, straight black hair that hung down over their round, gray faces, covering their eyes.

"Why are the others afraid of them?" Becca asked. "They're like little schoolboys or something."

"Look at their mouths," Serge said.

Even from a distance, it was easy to see their mouths were larger than normal, long, jagged grins that ran from ear to ear. Crossing their lips were thick, heavy stitches that keep their mouths tightly closed.

The triplets walked to the end of the side street and made a perfect synchronized right turn onto Orville Avenue. Every single monster, no matter how gruesome, gave them plenty of room as they passed.

"I've seen enough scary movies to know that we don't want to tick them off," Mason said.

"All right." Mari tore her gaze away from the window. "I think the coast is clear out back. We need to get going if—"

A heavy *thump* echoed through the empty house.

"What was that?" Becca said, her voice filled with terror.

"Maybe a cat or something," Mari said.

Thump.

All four of them jumped. Serge stepped toward the stairs and peered up.

109

"No way," Mason said, feeling a fresh surge of dread. "That wasn't a cat."

"It sounds like it's coming from upstairs," Becca said.

Thump.

"Let me check it out," Serge said.

"Are you crazy?" Mason said. "You don't go *check it out.* Never *check it out.*"

"Well, what do you suggest?" Serge asked.

"Maybe you could stop arguing," Mari replied.

"Maybe you could—"

"Guys!" Becca pointed up the stairs. They all turned. A man stood on the second-floor landing. No one spoke for several moments. They only stared at the stranger, who stood facing the wall. All at once, the man leaned back, then slammed his head against the wall.

Thump.

"Why's he doing that?" Mason squeaked. His voice was barely louder than a whisper, but it was enough to make the man turn and look at them. When he took a step forward, his face was finally visible in a sliver of moonlight. A ragged hunk of skin dangled from where the bottom lip should have been, revealing grimy, rotting teeth. Its eyes had gone a sickly yellow, like egg yolks about to burst. It was, Mason knew, impossible for those dead eyes to see anything at all, and yet the creature knew they were there.

"Zombie," Mason breathed.

The zombie's head tilted and it sniffed the air. The awful mouth creaked open, and it moaned loudly as it began to stumble down the stairs toward them, arms outstretched.

"Run!" Mason yelled.

They started back toward the kitchen, only to find a dozen sets of dead eyes gleaming in the darkness. The house was overrun with zombies. They must have been in the other rooms, sleeping perhaps, waiting for their turn to either give out treats or lumber forth in search of them. A woman in a filthy purple dress near the front of the pack reached for Mason. Her hand brushed against his arm and one of her fingers broke off with a dry snap. It fell to the linoleum floor just as Mason started to scream. He turned and kicked hard into the dead woman's stomach. The dead woman's balance seemed nonexistent, and she fell backward into the crowd.

"We have to go!"

"Where?" Serge yelled.

The four of them backed toward the stairs as the zombies pressed in around them. They couldn't go out front. They were surrounded now, but that was nothing compared to the horde of monsters outside. The zombies were slow at least, and easier to handle from the looks of it.

They always are, he thought, *until there are too many of them, and they overrun you and then they start to tear you to pieces. . . .*

"Upstairs!" Mari said.

"But . . . what about—"

"I got him," Serge said, somehow sounding both annoyed and terrified at the same time. He leapt halfway up the stairs and swung the bat into the side of the first zombie's head hard enough to send it tumbling over the rail to splat on the floor between Mason and Becca. They ran upstairs in a group, trying to put space between them and the growling moans that chased them, nipping at their heels.

"Here," Serge said, running into the nearest bedroom. In a few seconds, he had flipped on the light, checked the closet, and peeked under the bed. "It's clear. Get in here."

Mason was the last one in, and after he slammed the door, he turned and yelled, feeling a fresh surge of panic. A face peered out of the mirror on the vanity on the opposite side of the room. The others saw it as well, and they scrambled to get away from what must have been another zombie that had snuck into the room earlier.

"Wait," Mari said. "It's not one of them. It's . . . Mr. Perkins?"

Mason squinted, and as ridiculous as it seemed, he saw the truth for himself. The face looking out of the mirror *was* Mr. Perkins's. He had been one of the maintenance men at the middle school until he retired. The old man was leaning into the mirror and combing his thin white hair. He wore a shiny vampire cape, and when he opened his mouth, he slapped in a pair of fake fangs. Then he smiled and growled at his own reflection before disappearing.

"What was that?" Becca asked.

"I . . . I don't know," Mari replied as she walked closer for a better look. She picked up a picture frame that sat on the vanity. "It's him," she said, holding the frame up for the others to see. Mason took it from her. The man in the photo was decades younger, his hair just starting to turn white, but there was no mistaking the maintenance man.

"We're in his house," Mason said. "The mirror is like a window or something. I think we're seeing into the real Pearl."

Beyond the closed door, the hallway was alive with shuffling feet and moaning voices. Serge slammed against the door and held it shut.

"This is all *very* interesting, but we don't have time for it," he said.

"Let's block the door," Mason said. "Buy us some time."

"We're stuck," Becca said, fear rising in her voice.

"Here," Mari said, looking out the window. "We can climb down."

Mason peered out and saw that it led out onto the roof. From there, it was only a short drop down to the back porch.

"Okay," Mason said, "I think we're going to be—"

The horde of zombies hit the door hard enough to nearly knock Serge down. He yelled, dug in his heels, and slammed one shoulder against the door. Rotting arms reached around the doorframe, grabbing for his face. One of them pulled off Serge's hat and receded back into the hall, and Mason was struck with the sudden image of a zombie wearing a baseball cap as it stumbled around town.

"Help me!" Serge yelled.

This was, as Mason knew, the crucial moment in any zombie movie. Make the right decision and escape or become zombie dinner. Mason's instincts told him to open the window, climb onto the roof, drop onto the back porch, and then run, keep running, never stopping until he was home. But this was *Serge*. This was the only guy in the world who really understood him. This was the guy who would throw himself into that horde of zombies to keep Mason safe. Even if it all ended right then and there, Mason couldn't leave him hanging.

He scanned the room in a split second and saw the two things he needed.

"Mari, Becca"—he pointed at the tall dresser next to the door—"get on the other side and be ready to tip it over."

The girls fell into position, and Mason ran to the vanity. He pushed the mirror off it, wincing as it shattered into hundreds of pieces, and pulled the small piece of furniture away from the wall.

Zombies are clumsy, he told himself, remembering how easily the woman in the kitchen had fallen over. *Please, let zombies be clumsy.*

The vanity slid smoothly across the wooden floor, and Mason lined it up on the opposite wall, directly in front of the door. He glanced at Serge, who nodded, picking up on his plan.

"When I start running," he said over the chorus of moans, "open the door."

"Okay," Serge said nervously.

"Be ready to close it, dude," Mason added.

"I got you." Serge flashed a strained smile. "You got this, Mason."

Mason looked at the girls. "As soon as he shuts the door, push the dresser over, okay?"

Mari nodded, and she and Becca started to tip it onto its side.

Mason took a deep breath and whispered, "Let's do it."

Then he started to push. It took a few steps to build up speed, but soon enough, he was a runaway train, screaming and flying toward Serge, who still held the door shut.

"Now!"

Serge rolled to the side, opening the door as he did so, and Mason saw them. Zombies covered the stairs like a plague of rats. Although it was impossible to say exactly how many had been lurking in the nooks and crannies of the house, there were easily at least thirty. It took everything Mason had to force himself to keep running into that meat grinder of teeth and rotten, grasping hands, but he did it. With a scream, he slammed the vanity into the zombie at the front of the pack, an old woman with a very large blue hat.

She was buried in that hat, Mason thought as the vanity slammed into her at the waist, doubling her over and sending her reeling backward down the stairs. Zombies fell and tumbled in a chorus of angry moans as they crashed into one another like bowling pins. Mason couldn't help but smile. It was a short victory, though. In mere seconds, the hole he had made in the crowd was refilling with decaying faces.

"Close the door!" he screamed, and Serge slammed it shut. A split second later, the girls pushed the dresser and it toppled over. Serge barely rolled out of the way in time to keep from being flattened.

The door was blocked, but Mason wasn't taking any chances. He grabbed the bedposts and began to pull, and the others joined him, slamming the bed into the dresser. The zombies thumped and beat on the door.

"See," Mason said as he breathed heavily. "I got this."

Serge smiled at him. "I guess you do."

Mari opened the window and peered out.

"Is Pumpkin Head out there?" Mason asked.

"I don't see him," she answered.

"Let's get out of here," Mason said. "That door won't hold forever."

He watched the door as the others slipped out into the night. Serge was already on the back porch by the time Mason joined Mari and Becca on the roof. One by one, they carefully lowered themselves to the ground. Mason went last, and as he was climbing down, he slipped and landed flat on his butt. It was a painful shock to his system, but he jumped back up quickly. "I'm fine. I'm good."

"Mason, I gotta say," Serge said, letting out a low whistle, "*that* was a plan."

"Um, yeah," Mari added. "I'm a little surprised that worked."

Mason smiled and took a deep, heavy breath. "Well, there's more where that came from." Mari rolled her eyes, and he immediately regretted saying something so stupid. "I mean . . . thanks. I couldn't have done it without all of you."

"So, what now?" Becca asked.

"Let's try this again," Mason said. "Mr. Kirby's house. Quick and quiet, right?"

Mari nodded. "That's the plan. The *next* plan."

CHAPTER 12

The Witch's Basement

After taking a few steps onto Orville Avenue, Meg wished she were still inside the scarecrow. The scene was almost indescribable. Nightmarish monsters were everywhere, and every single one stopped and smiled when they saw her coming.

"Is this the one?" a voice called.

"Oh, it must be."

"She'll do lovely."

"Let me see, I want to *see*. . . ."

She was surrounded by leering faces, glowing eyes, claws that clicked on the pavement, mouths that opened in fanged smiles and blew billows of rotten breath in Meg's direction. There was nowhere to go, nowhere to hide, so she reached for the most human thing around her. She clung to Ms. Vernon's waist and buried her face into the folds of her cloak.

"Step back," Ms. Vernon said in a loud, commanding voice. "You'll all get what you want, but please, make room."

A creature that could only be described as a frog man waddled forward, his massive feet slapping the pavement. Meg glanced up for only a moment, just long enough to see his wart-covered face and lolling tongue.

"Why, Serpa, she looks *delectable*," he said in a watery voice. "Please, accept this."

He held out a small, smudged jar filled with yellow liquid. Something pale floated inside the jar, and as it drifted around, she could see what looked like toenails.

"Are those pickled toes?" Ms. Vernon asked kindly. "Wherever did you find them?"

"Don't you worry about that. It's worth it for all your fine work."

"Please drop them off with the Skinless on the porch, and thank you for your courtesy."

The Skinless? Meg thought with a shiver. Her mind filled with images too gruesome to say aloud. The monsters were still murmuring among themselves as she and Ms. Vernon passed, but she refused to look up. Instead, she walked awkwardly, letting Ms. Vernon guide her. She had no clue where they were, but a few moments later, the witch said, "Watch the steps."

Meg pulled away long enough to see the wooden steps leading up to the same porch where Ms. Vernon had been standing earlier.

We're back at her house, Meg thought. *Home is just down the street.*

The realization filled her equally with hope and dread. It was nice to think that she was so close to her home and, more importantly, her parents, but it was clear that this town belonged to the monsters now. Meg shuddered to think what might have happened to her mom and dad.

And Mason too.

The thought of her brother made her heart ache. She could still see him in her mind, reaching for her, looking somehow more afraid than she was. Everything that had felt wrong over the past year or two seemed to melt away, leaving only the truth behind, like a snowman's hat left after the sun has melted everything else. Mason was her big brother, and he would do anything for her. They loved each other, and the thought that she might never see him again was enough to turn her heart into brittle glass.

Ms. Vernon opened the door and ushered her inside the house by tapping her cane on Meg's back. The foul wooden face on the end of the cane twisted into a smile, and Meg stepped forward, avoiding its touch. She stood in a small living room decorated with dark wood furniture and deep-red curtains. She scanned the room and registered the small details: the rolltop desk, the feather quill stuck in a brass inkpot, the bundle of dead flowers in a vase, the framed black-and-white pictures. In the presence of the witch, it all seemed eerie and surreal, but in another way, it almost looked cozy. When the door closed, Meg realized that she and Ms. Vernon were finally alone. She wondered, vaguely, whether she should make a run for it.

"Let's get a few things out of the way up front," Ms.

Vernon said. "If you try to escape, I'll melt your feet." It was as though the witch was reading her mind.

Don't think, Meg thought. *Just clear your head.*

"I've done it before, you know," Ms. Vernon continued. "Melted feet, that is. The skin falls right off the bones like warm caramel. It won't kill you, but it will be beyond painful. And I'll make you keep walking too." She said it in a way that let Meg know it was true, and when she shivered, the face on the witch's cane laughed.

Now all I can think about is caramel feet.

Ms. Vernon walked to a corner of the room where a thin, circular table stood. It was ornately carved from dark wood and matched the floor. The top was small, no larger than a dinner plate, and Meg thought it might have been used at some point to display a vase filled with flowers. The witch picked the table up and carried it across the room, to a spot near the center. A few small scuff marks decorated the floor, and Ms. Vernon carefully arranged the table directly on top of them.

What is she doing?

Ms. Vernon took a step back, surveying her work. Then she walked over to the rolltop desk near the front door and slid open its cover. Inside was a large crystal bowl. She picked it up carefully with both hands and set it upon the small table.

"As you may have guessed," she said as she nudged the bowl into position, "I have little use for children and even less patience."

She pushed the bowl a bit to one side, studying the position of it carefully.

"But we all have jobs to do," she continued. "Your job is remarkably simple. Just do whatever I say, and you'll be fine."

"What do you want me to do?" Meg asked.

Ms. Vernon raised one eyebrow. "I don't like children, but I *especially* don't like talkative children. My own son was talkative. He learned."

"I'm sorry. I just . . . I'll do whatever you need me to."

The raised eyebrow smoothed out, and Ms. Vernon turned back to the table.

"That's good to hear," she said, and gave a quick nod, satisfied with her strange furniture rearrangement. "Follow me."

Meg trailed behind her down the dimly lit hall. Just then, a small creature appeared at the far end of the hall and began walking toward them. It was small, shorter even than Meg, and each footstep made a light slapping sound. The sound reminded Meg of a piece of raw chicken being dropped on the kitchen floor. A few moments later, the creature emerged into the light, and Meg had to cover her mouth with both hands to keep from screaming.

Skinless, she thought.

The little creature looked like a piece of raw meat with two beady eyes and a tiny, smiling mouth. Its arms and legs were short and stubby, and its body was rounder in the middle, ending in a small, narrow head.

"Hold the door for us," Ms. Vernon said. "And wake the others. They'll need to start handing out the candy soon."

Skinless smiled, and despite how awful it looked, Meg found it oddly cute. It bobbed over to a door in the center of the hallway and pulled it open, its stubby hands just barely reaching the knob. The door swung wide, and a smell like old books rushed out, filling Meg's nostrils.

"Go on," Ms. Vernon said.

Meg walked to the threshold and looked in.

The stairs led downward, into a darkened place beneath their feet.

"I don't want to."

The little Skinless shot a nervous look from Meg to Ms. Vernon.

"You're not making a good first impression," Ms. Vernon said. "What was your name again?"

"Meg."

"Well, Meg, if you'd rather lose those feet . . ."

"No!" Meg said. "It's just . . . it's just dark is all."

Ms. Vernon held up her cane and tapped it on the floor. The face smiled, and lights bloomed to life.

"Better?"

Meg went down the staircase without another word. When she reached the bottom, overhead lights popped on, illuminating walls draped with resplendent purple fabric. A fine, deep-red rug covered the floor. Wooden shelves and tables lined with all sorts of odd objects filled the room. Tiny cages containing thin skeletons. Jars of colorful liquids with eyes or fingers floating inside.

Meg wished the lights weren't on.

The monsters bring her all this stuff, she thought, remembering the frog man. *For her spells.*

In the center of the room was a stout, heavy chair with metal clamps on its arms and legs. A grim-looking metal bowl hovered over the top of the chair. Even though she had never seen one in person, Meg knew exactly what it was. She'd seen an electric chair in one of Mason's horror movies, and she could still remember how the murderer had screamed when they turned up the voltage.

She can't make me go in there.

Meg was mistaken. The witch had a way about her, a will that extended far beyond magic and spells, and she seemed to always know what Meg was thinking before she even had a chance to think it.

"Magic is an interesting thing," the witch said. She stood about a foot or so away from Meg. "It's fickle and delicate. If you do the wrong thing, you can kill a spell before it starts, but if you can figure out how to harness it, there's no limit to what you can do. Even witches need a bit of help sometimes."

She held her cane a few inches from Meg's nose. The awful little face grinned dumbly.

"This is no ordinary cane," she said. "I was married to a buffoon once. Killing him would have been immensely easy but also very wasteful. Human souls are wonderful conductors for magic. And if you ask me, he's much happier now."

The cane's eyes opened wider, and they began to glow as if the carving were filled with embers.

"Sit," the witch commanded.

Meg's mind refused, but her body obeyed. She walked up and dropped onto the hard, unfeeling chair. The moment she felt the solid, unflinching wood, Meg knew the electric chair was real. The witch whispered a few short words and, without using her hands, the metal clamps slammed shut.

This is it, Meg thought. *This is how I die.*

She was quietly sobbing by then, and the witch looked down at her with disdain.

"Stop that," she said, brushing bone-white hair from her face. "I have zero patience for whining. Do you honestly think I'd bring you all the way here just to shock you to death?"

Meg felt weak and exhausted, but the witch's expression demanded an answer.

"I guess not."

"Humph. Give me a bit of credit. If I wanted you dead, I'd snap my fingers and watch you curl up like a bug. Or I'd have one of those monsters sneak into your house and gobble you up. It would be *beneath me* to do something so . . . pedestrian. Do you understand?"

Meg didn't, but she nodded all the same.

"Just sit there," the witch said as she turned toward the stairs. "The chair might not be comfy, but it has a bit of a *memory* to it. Makes the spell run smoother." She chuckled as if she had just told a remarkably funny joke, then added, "I've done all the hard work. Your part is easy. Just sit. Relax. You'll be *fine.*"

There wasn't an ounce of genuine reassurance in her voice, but Meg did as she was told. The witch left the basement, and Meg listened, counting her steps up the stairs, followed by the slam of the door. She was alone, and she sat in silence for a very long time, though she couldn't guess exactly how long. She was awash in a feeling of odd separation, like she was watching herself in a movie.

It was impossible to say how long she waited, but all at

once, Meg felt something tugging at her, pulling her hair upward toward the ceiling. It felt like static electricity, the way her hair stood up when she rubbed a balloon on her head and then lifted it. The drag on her body eventually pulled her gaze up toward the ceiling.

"Oh my . . ."

The ceiling was covered with black markings, a series of concentric circles and strange, otherworldly symbols.

I bet that's a spell, Meg thought, and a moment later, the symbols began to move. It was subtle at first, but the sensation that the space above her was no longer solid grew and grew. The drywall had turned to white paste and something was churning it from underneath. She couldn't drag her eyes away from the sight. She could only stare, caught in the moment like a mouse gazing into a cat's green eyes. Soon, colors appeared, little drops of orange and black that mingled, grew, and curled into the center. The ceiling had blurred into a vortex that was drawing her ever closer. It made her lightheaded, but somehow, it felt *good.*

It's pretty, she thought, her eyes still cast upward. Meg let herself drift.

CHAPTER 13

Becca's Home Run

"All right," Mason said, "just one more block and we're there."

Ever since leaving the zombie house, they had followed a simple but effective plan. Hug the tree line. Move quickly. Stay quiet. They could still hear the raucous monsters and occasionally see them through the gaps between houses, but they were able to stick to the shadows and stay undetected.

The group slowed their steady jog to a walk as they approached a huge oak tree. When they reached it, almost as one, they leaned against it to catch their breath.

Mason rested his hands on his knees, and when he glanced over at the others, he saw that he wasn't the only one who was struggling. Becca had slumped against the tree.

"I don't feel so good," she mumbled, swaying back and forth.

Serge must have seen what was coming, because he was there to catch her as she passed out.

"What's wrong with her? Is she like diabetic or something?" Mason asked, alarmed.

"No," Mari said, and Mason could hear the panic in her voice. "But maybe it's stress? She doesn't do great with stress."

"Whoa," Serge said, "I got you." He set Becca carefully on the ground, propping her back up against the tree.

"Does anyone have a paper bag she can breathe into?" Mason asked as Mari fanned Becca's face with her hand.

Serge looked up at him.

"What?" Mason said defensively. "I saw it in a movie once."

A few seconds later, Becca's eyes fluttered open, and she sat up, looking more embarrassed than anything.

"What happened?" she asked.

"You fainted," Serge replied. "I was . . . a little worried."

"Oh my gosh." She turned red under the zombie makeup. "That's so embarrassing."

"It's understandable . . . you know . . . considering."

They smiled at each other, and Mason had a quick, vaguely horrifying vision of sappy music playing as the two of them leaned in for an even sappier kiss.

Instead, the branch right above them moved, and a handful of dead leaves rained down on them. Mason looked up, right into the green eyes and horrid grin of the scarecrow.

With a single swipe, the scarecrow reached down and lifted Serge off the ground by one arm. The baseball bat tumbled from Serge's hands and landed uselessly by Becca's feet.

The scarecrow lowered himself to the ground and pushed Serge against the tree. The roots of his hands crackled as they grew, enveloping Serge in vines and pinning him to the tree trunk.

"Do something!" Mari yelled.

Mason moved to get the bat. As he did, the scarecrow took his free hand and swatted Mari to the ground, before doing the same to Mason. Mason fell backward, landing hard. The scarecrow glowered down at Becca, seeming to speak without saying a single word.

What are you going to do?

Becca wasn't a threat, and the scarecrow knew it. He turned away from her and continued encasing Serge in vines.

"Help me," Serge wheezed. "I can't get out. . . ."

"Where's the bat?" Mason screamed, and turned just in time to see Becca rushing the scarecrow, baseball bat in hand.

"Hey!" she yelled at the scarecrow. "I'm talking to you!" The bat was shaking in her hands, and her voice, though trembling, was loud and strong. Fear had changed her, turned her into something fierce and dangerous.

With a running leap, Becca swung. The bat caught the pumpkin on one cheek, and it burst open in a spray of orange bits. He turned away from Serge, who was still pinned to the tree, and with a *whoosh* the flames inside his pumpkin head billowed out of the hole.

With a wild scream, Becca swung again.

The bat smacked against the head, this time taking a huge chunk off the right side of the pumpkin. The third swing caved in the nose and half of the mouth. The fourth took the stem and cap clean off. But it was the fifth swing that knocked the entire pumpkin off the scarecrow's spindly shoulders. The pumpkin's husk tumbled and rolled a few feet before lodging itself up against a tree.

"I did it," Becca muttered, eyes blazing. "I killed it."

The scarecrow stood unmoving for a moment.

Mason expected the shoulders to slump, the arms to go slack, and the entire body to drop to the ground in a final spasm. Instead, the space where the head had been began to glow. The scarecrow had a thin, sharp wooden neck, and the green fire sparked up once again, hovering in the air where the pumpkin had been. A second later, one gnarled hand shot forward and grabbed Becca by the neck. An explosion of vines grew out of the hand, wrapping her up the same as Serge.

"Why are you trapping them?" a cold voice cried from overhead. "I thought I made myself very clear."

Mason looked up and saw a strange, solid-white bird sitting high up in the branches. It stared down at them with blood-red eyes.

"I ordered you to *kill*," the bird said.

The scarecrow's shoulders slumped. He looked almost guilty, like a kid getting yelled at by a teacher.

He doesn't want to kill, Mason thought, a spark of hope igniting in him.

129

"This is your last chance," the bird called. For a brief second, the scarecrow turned toward Becca, who closed her eyes, expecting the worst. Instead, the scarecrow's vines receded as he set the terrified girl back on the ground.

"Very well," the bird said.

The scarecrow's body spasmed painfully, and the fire that had filled its pumpkin head sputtered and faded before the tall frame dropped to the ground, lifeless.

The bird cawed loudly and fluttered down to a lower branch as Becca and Mari helped Serge break out of the vines that encased him.

"You're trespassing," the bird said directly to Mason. "Then again, what else would I expect from *children*?"

It spat out the word *children,* as if it tasted bad.

It's her, Mason thought, staring into those deep red pits for eyes. *The Red Witch of Pearl.*

"I've always hated children. Before I found the secrets of the darkness, they told me I'd make a good wife for some local fool who had chosen me. Henry was his name, and he was quite the oaf. I was too weak in those days to say no, but I managed to make the best of . . . *marriage.* And I even found a use for Henry. After all these years, I still keep him very close."

"It's her," Mason whispered to the others.

"Yes," the crow said. "It's me. I assume you stumbled onto this place looking for the girl. Meg . . . is that her name?"

"Please," Mason said, "give her back." Mari put a hand on his arm.

"Coming here was very brave. I do admire your hearts. I'll

make sure to hang onto them after I'm done with the rest of you."

Anger swirled up so hot that Mason could feel his face going red. Mari tried to pull him back, but he twisted away.

"Look at that smashed-up pumpkin," he said, pointing at the remains of the scarecrow. "Is that the best you got? I hope not, 'cause we're just getting started." His voice was shaking with fear, but he somehow managed to get the words out.

The witch-crow let out a deep, genuine laugh that melted into a series of long caws. "Mr. Crow was getting soft in his old age," she said. "A monster with a conscience is a pitiful thing. Don't you worry, though; we've got plenty of others interested in taking his job. I've forgotten how entertaining it can be for things to go wrong. There's true joy to be had in dealing with the little mistakes that pop up. Rest assured, you'll all be dead soon, but know that you've already made this a *deliciously* memorable year. I might even use what's left of you for next year. You know," she said as she hopped down to a lower branch, "I have a method for turning children into little skinless creatures. They don't talk, but that just means they don't talk back. You'd be a lot more useful that way. Or maybe I could—"

"Enough," Mari said. "Just leave us alone."

The crow tilted its head.

"You know, for as long as I've lived here, I haven't really paid much attention to the boring humans that walk around these streets. But you . . ."

The crow hopped down yet again.

"I recognize *you*. The building on the corner. Third floor. Big window. Always up there, reading a book."

"No," Mari whispered.

"*Yes.* I see you up there on my walks. Who knows . . . I might even give you, or your *family*, a visit."

The bird leapt up and away, cawing and laughing as it went.

Mason turned to look at Mari and realized Becca and Serge were looking at her as well, as if they were all holding their breath, waiting for her to say something.

"I need to get out of here," she said finally, eyes wild with terror.

"Just breathe," Becca said.

"She knows where I live!" Mari cried. "Where I *sleep*! What if my mom comes home? What if the witch sends someone . . . *some* . . . *thing* to hurt her?"

"It doesn't change the plan," Mason said.

"I don't care about your plan! Not until I know my mom is safe."

"Wait a second," Becca said. "The mirrors! Mr. Perkins's house! We can see into the real world through them."

"You're right," Mari said, understanding dawning on her face.

"Wait," Serge said, "what good will that do?"

"I can at least check my house," Mari said. "See if my mom's there. Make sure she's safe."

Mason shook his head. "What if you see something you don't want to—"

"Then we'll deal with it!" she said. "Look, we've been helping you all night. I don't think it's asking too much for you to help me. My apartment isn't far from here. And . . . if no one else agrees, I'll go alone."

"No," Mason said. "You don't have to do it alone. We'll find a way to check on your mom. I just don't know how."

A long moment of awkward silence fell, and it was broken by a giggle. Gloom was standing right beside them, looking down at Mr. Crow's pitiful remains.

"That's one monster down," she said with a laugh. "At this rate, you'll probably save your sister just in time for Christmas."

"One dead monster is better than nothing," Mason snapped.

"Hmm . . . maybe," Gloom said, leaning down and touching the scarecrow's wooden shoulder. "Like I said, near-death experiences are sort of my thing. Well, technically *full-death* experiences are my thing. Making life isn't easy, but making death isn't as simple as some people think. This big guy might have some fight left in him."

She ran a bony finger over the scarecrow's shoulder, and he shuddered slightly.

"That's the thing about witches," Gloom said. "Serpa brought this one to life, and she thought it would be just as easy to take that away. But life is a tricky thing. It's stubborn. It fights to survive. Even when every rational fiber of being tells it to let go . . . life just *hangs on.*"

The fire where the scarecrow's head had once been

suddenly sputtered back to life like a trick birthday candle. Mason screamed, his heart pounding, and leapt back, behind Becca, who lifted the bat once again.

"Why would you do that?" Mason yelled.

"Hey, don't blame me," Gloom said. "I just work here."

She patted the headless scarecrow on the shoulder, and he sat up, curling his knees into his chest and wrapping his long arms around them. "There's a nice lesson here, though," she said. "This witch doesn't know how vulnerable she is. No one has opposed her for a very long time, and as clever as she can be, all that confidence has made her careless. Even now, she's put all her eggs in one basket."

"What do you mean?" Mason asked, still eyeing the scarecrow.

"The curse on Pearl," Gloom said. "This copy of a town. The way people forget. It's all *one spell*, and it takes a lot to keep a spell like that going. Remember when I said every spell is a living thing? Well, it lives *and* dies, sometimes in the span of less than a second. That's why women make the best witches. They're not just raising magic out of thin air . . . they're giving birth to the thing. Serpa might hate children, but this spell is her true child, maybe the only thing in the world she actually loves. It takes some serious energy to keep alive, even for a single night. To keep it stable. To keep the blood of the spell pumping. And what a huge, intricate spell like this needs is a *heart*, a physical object she can pour all that magic into. A spell with a heart can last a lot longer than a spell without one."

Mason shook his head. "I don't understand what you're saying."

Gloom gazed at him. "I'm saying, do you want to find your sister? Or do you want to end this for good?"

Serge stood and brushed bits of vine off his shoulders. "We have to get Meg and get out of here," he said.

"I know that's your answer," Gloom said before nodding at Becca and Mari. "And I'm sure you two would say the same. But you"—she pointed a long, thin finger at Mason—"what do you have to say?"

A memory flashed into Mason's mind of him and Marco sitting on the floor of his bedroom, talking about monsters, plotting out the movies they'd make once they were old enough. Mason could remember when he first got the notepad out of his desk and started writing the story. Their story.

"We have to stop it," Mason said. "All of it. We have to try."

"Then find the heart of the spell and destroy it," Gloom said.

"So, what, do we have to kill her and take it out of her pocket?" Becca asked.

"The magic in the heart radiates outward . . . I'm guessing it's something small hidden near the middle of town," Gloom said as she absent-mindedly dug around in her bag. "If I were you, I'd look there." She fished out another handmade doll and squinted at it. This one was a woman with wild blond hair, a red dress, and a vampire's painted face.

"Busy night," Gloom said as she walked behind the tree and disappeared.

"We have to get to my mom," Mari said, her voice more panicked than it had been before.

"Wait," Becca said, pointing. "What about him?"

The giant, headless scarecrow was leaning against the tree, and he seemed to be making himself as small as possible, like a stray cat trying to hide from the people attempting to help him.

"He's pathetic," Mari said.

"Well, I hope he learned his lesson," Mason said. "Just leave him here. We have to get moving."

The group took a few steps, and the headless scarecrow scrambled to his feet, bobbing along behind them like a toddler chasing a dog that refuses to play.

"This isn't going to work," Mari said. "We can't sneak around with him following us."

"Oh, for crying out loud," Mason said as he marched back toward the scarecrow. "What do you want?"

The scarecrow held his hands up in a clear sign of confusion.

"Look, *you're* the bad guy," Mason said. "*We're* the good guys. You almost killed us, remember?"

The scarecrow pointed at himself, as if the fact that he worked for the witch was news to him.

"Yes! You."

The broad shoulders slumped, and the scarecrow looked absolutely pitiful. He started to slink away, but Serge stepped forward.

"You saw how the witch treated him," Serge said.

"Yeah," Mason said. "What about it?"

"Just hear me out here, and don't freak out, but . . . maybe he's not so bad."

"Not so bad?" Becca repeated, her jaw dropping.

"He could have killed me," Serge said. "You too," he added, pointing at Becca. "But he didn't. He stood up to her even though he knew what would happen if he did."

The others didn't look convinced, but Serge turned to the scarecrow.

"Mr. Crow?" Serge asked. "That's your name, right?"

Even without a head, the scarecrow was able to nod by bending his body forward.

"What do you want from us?"

With a nervous twitch, he raised his hands and pointed to the spot where his head used to be.

"You want us to get you a new head?" Mason asked.

Mr. Crow gave them a thumbs-up.

Mason looked over at Serge, who grinned at him.

"I gotta say," Serge said, "having a monster on our side might be helpful."

Mason considered the idea, not quite letting on how exciting he thought having his own monster might be.

"Think about it like this," Serge continued. "He's gotta know where Meg is. If we help him out, he can help us out. Plus, I dunno . . . he might not be so bad if someone gave him a chance."

Mason turned back to Mr. Crow. "Okay, here's the deal. If

we get you a new head, you help find my sister. You do know where she is, don't you?"

The big, creaking hand made a big, creaking thumbs-up.

"All right then, Mr. Crow. It's a deal."

The gangly body jumped up and down, as excited as a little kid on Christmas morning. Or Halloween night.

CHAPTER 14

Welcome to the Team

"I'm sure you'll be happy to hear that we've recently had an opening on the team."

The witch was standing in her living room, speaking to the werewolf crouched in front of her couch. He was a tall, lithe creature, all legs and fur, less a wolf and more a giant greyhound. In the dim room, his jet-black fur almost seemed to drink the scant light, turning him into little more than a dark splotch with bright-yellow eyes.

"For the first time since we've started this little enterprise, some humans have stumbled into this place."

The wolf growled.

"I'm as shocked as you. Mr. Crow was . . . well, a disappointment. I *always* had doubts about him, you know."

The werewolf's lips pulled back over his teeth as he snarled softly.

"When you're right, you're right," the witch replied.

In the middle of the room, directly over the spot in the basement where Meg still sat, was the small, ornate wooden end table. The crystal bowl was still perched in the center.

"Hindsight is a powerful thing," she said as she fished a blood-red handkerchief from a hidden pocket. The wolf growled once more. "I have a lot of creatures I can call on, but I believe you'd be especially adept at handling this . . . issue."

The witch covered the bowl carefully with the handkerchief and closed her eyes, whispering a few words. The cane leaning in the corner opened its mouth like a fish sucking in water. A moment later, she removed the cloth. The bowl was filled with dozens of pieces of candy, neat little pucks about the size of quarters and perfectly wrapped in bright black-and-orange paper.

"Playing human for one night a year is good fun, but for a monster like you, I think I have something even better."

Picking up the bowl, Serpa walked to the front door and opened it. The Skinless was standing on the other side, waiting patiently and holding a burlap sack. When it saw her, the odd little creature held the sack out.

"Distribute these," she said, emptying the bowl into the bag.

The creature nodded courteously and waddled away. Before she could close the door, an identical little creature had taken its place, and it too smiled blankly as it waited for the bowl to refill. Ms. Vernon closed the door on it and returned to the living room, setting the bowl back in its place.

"There are four children in here with us," she said. "I know where one of them lives. I'd like you to visit her apartment on the corner of Orville and Banner Street. It's a brick building, three stories tall. I'm sure you'll be able to find it."

Her cane began to mumble softly, and Serpa held it to her ear.

"Oh, Henry," she whispered. "I don't think we need to do *that*."

She turned her attention back to the wolf. "I'm sure you'll find some family. Mother. Father. Maybe even siblings."

She gave the cane a gentle kiss on top of its head. The face smiled.

"I've had so many disappointments in my life," Serpa said to the wolf. "My child, my husband, even my dear departed sisters."

Serpa pushed her lower lip out and made an exaggerated sad face.

"I've put them *all* to a good use, because I hate being disappointed. You wouldn't disappoint me, would you?"

The wolf growled, long and deep, and Serpa smiled.

"Good boy. Go to the girl's house. Kill whoever you find and bring me back a souvenir. Something the girl will recognize."

Ms. Vernon opened the door, and the wolf curled itself through the opening like a cat.

"Do well and you'll be my second-in-command, with all the perks included, of course," she called as the wolf dashed off into the night, howling as it went. Ms. Vernon glanced over at the empty bowl. It was time to fill it once more.

CHAPTER 15

Mouths to Feed

Meg was floating.

She was still sitting in the hard chair, still locked in the witch's basement, still occasionally glancing up at the melty, goopy ceiling, but she was also floating. Time was a meaningless, distant thing that didn't seem to apply to her any longer. It felt like the room itself wasn't really a room in an old lady's basement. Instead, it too was floating in some endless void where time no longer existed. It wasn't a pleasant thought, endlessly existing, never fully asleep or awake, just drifting as if she had had too much cough syrup and a bad fever. Then again, she wasn't really afraid either. She felt as if she were *past* being afraid. Fear felt like a thing she'd outgrown somehow, the same way she'd let her mom put a box of toys in the attic the year before.

She might have drifted in that place forever, like a leaf on the surface of a still pond, and that would have been just fine with her. It certainly would have been better than what happened next.

The first inkling of the change started in the soft fold of skin at her elbow. At first, Meg thought that maybe she had slipped down in the chair and caught her arm at a weird angle. Or maybe she had pinched herself in the cracked wooden armrest. She looked down and, to her surprise, saw that her arms hadn't moved.

And yet, the pain was still there.

It was slight at first, almost gentle, like a small set of fingers pinching her. But a few seconds later, the sensation deepened, and the pain was suddenly bright and clear. It was teeth she felt. Of that, there was no question.

"Ow!" Meg yelled, though there was no one to hear her.

The feeling faded a moment later, and she went back to floating calmly, that draining feeling drawing her upward, like a bathtub drain that circled up instead of down.

The next bite was on her ankle. This one was immediate, the teeth sharp and hungry. There was another bite on her neck, but those teeth felt square and heavy, like the cow's teeth she'd seen on her class's last field trip. She remembered wondering what those flat teeth would feel like if she accidentally stuck her finger between them. Now she knew. Another bite caught her lower back, but this one felt as if it had no teeth at all, like a fish's mouth. She had the mental image of a large gummy bear attacking her.

Soon, there were too many bites to count, too many to separate. Her body was alive with the sense of being eaten by countless tiny mouths all at once, and the only respite was that with each new bite, she felt them less and less. The upside-down drain over her head was pulling her higher and higher, and with each passing second, she was only dimly aware of the teeth.

Meg was glad not to feel them, but she was also struck by a deeply awful image. She imagined a birthday cake sitting on a table in a dark room. In the shadows, dozens of glowing eyes—*monster eyes*—were staring down at the cake. It was shaped like a little girl dressed as a princess in a blue dress. The monsters were very hungry, and Meg knew the cake wouldn't last long. A single question remained in her mind, bright as a filament inside a light bulb.

When the cake was devoured and gone, what would be left of the little girl?

CHAPTER 16

The Personality Transplant

The group was crouched in the backyard of a house a block from Mr. Kirby's. They huddled in patches of shadow, the monsters parading on the street just out of sight.

"I'll do it," Serge said.

"Come on, it should be me," Mason said.

"I'm the one who took care of the scarecrow." Becca swung the bat around and caught herself on the back of the head. Mason laughed, but Serge only smiled. There was no denying it. Before, it had just been flirting and goofy banter, but now Mason knew. Serge was head over heels. He tried to pretend that he didn't feel a pang of jealousy, but that would have been a lie.

"Yeah, you did," Serge said smiling.

"But it's fine," Becca said. "You and Mason go. Just be careful."

"And make sure you get a good one," Mari added.

"This is Mr. and Mrs. Jenkins's house," Serge said confidently. "They don't do bad ones."

"What I mean is, try to go for something a little more . . . well, friendly."

"Don't worry," Mason said. "We'll get a good one."

They ran through the dark backyard, careful of the doghouse next door. A moment later, Mason realized there was no dog, not in UnderPearl, and he laughed.

"What?" Serge whispered.

"Nothing. Come on."

They clung to the shadows, staying close to the house but careful not to catch the attention of any monsters that might be inside. The front porch had a wraparound railing that was surrounded by shrubs, and Mason knew there would be plenty of jack-o'-lanterns to pick from. He motioned for Serge to wait and dropped to his hands and knees. He crawled, staying low behind the shrubs that bordered the porch. The sounds of walking, talking, and growling monsters was all around him, and Mason wondered briefly if any of this was worth the trouble. He crept forward and looked up, spotting a good-sized jack-o'-lantern on the railing above him. Quick as a rabbit, he reached up and grabbed it, then crawled back to Serge.

Crouched in the shadows, he held the pumpkin up for Serge to see.

"Uh, no," Serge said. Mason turned the pumpkin around and groaned inwardly. The carved mouth looked as though it were melting, the teeth like jagged knives, and the angry eyes swirled with fire. Somehow, it was more terrifying than the first pumpkin head.

"Hang on." Mason scurried back and grabbed another pumpkin. "This might be about as good as it gets," he said, panting from the extra trip.

He held the pumpkin up and Serge's eyebrows shot up.

"Well . . . it's definitely friendlier."

They returned to the backyard and Serge held the pumpkin behind his back.

"Keep in mind," he said, "that we didn't have a ton to choose from."

"Just hand it over," Mari said, and when Serge did, Mari turned to Mr. Crow. "Okay, lean down. I'll try to be gentle."

The scarecrow creaked and popped as he slowly lowered his neck, which jutted out like a wooden stake that had been carved to slay a vampire. Mari squinted and carefully lined up her shot. Then she jammed the pumpkin down on the end of the stake. Mason held his breath. For a moment, nothing happened. Then, the jack-o'-lantern filled with bubbling green fire, and Mr. Crow stood tall above them.

"Wow," Mason said. "That's . . . quite a change."

The eyes were huge and cartoonish, complete with glistening pupils that looked to Mason like they belonged on an anime character. The nose was a chunky triangle, and the mouth a huge friendly grin. The monster that had terrorized them mere hours ago was now the least threatening creature on the block.

"All right, Mr. Crow," Mari said. "Feeling better?"

The scarecrow stared out into the distance as his pumpkin

head boiled with green flame. For a split second, Mason thought they had made a mistake. The creature was whole once again, and he could certainly finish what he'd started if he wanted to. Mason glanced over at Serge. To his surprise, his friend didn't look scared.

"Hey," Serge said as Mr. Crow leaned down to his level. "That witch . . . she made you right?" Mr. Crow nodded. "So, she's kinda like your mom. You know, sometimes kids have to do what *they* think is right, you understand?"

The friendly pumpkin head nodded up and down excitedly. All four kids couldn't help but smile.

"Well, now that we've got some backup," Becca said, "where to next?"

"We still need to check Mr. Kirby's house," Mason said. "Otherwise, we're fighting a witch with nothing but bad language."

"And we need to check on my mom," Mari added.

"Right," Mason said, turning toward the street. The night was growing colder, and the air was as still as death. They could hear the crowd in the distance getting wilder. A blood-curdling shriek was silenced by what sounded eerily like a growling chain saw, which was then followed by a bellowing laugh. On and on it went, an endless cacophony of madness. Mason looked around, then glanced over at the Jenkins's house. It was a single-story home, and the roof was only about ten feet high.

"Hey"—he pointed at Mr. Crow—"you think you can get us up there?"

The scarecrow easily hoisted them up, one at a time. Mason waited for the others before he crept up to the point of the roof and peered over. His friends joined him, and the four stared down in silent, horrified disbelief. Every square inch of the street was filled with a different type of monster, some less than a foot tall and others more than ten. It was like a scene out of a horror movie, nightmares coming alive and stalking the streets. Most of them were smiling and laughing, but that somehow made it more frightening. They were clearly having the time of their lives.

"Look," Mason said, pointing. In the world of colorful madness, Mr. Kirby's house stood out like a lump of coal. It was half a block down, on the opposite side of the street. The lights were out, and the yard was completely bare, not a decoration in sight.

"It's right there," Serge said.

"It might as well be on Mars." Becca sighed.

"You can't see it, but my apartment building is just on the other side of the old hardware store," Mari said. "It would take only two minutes to run there."

"And thirty seconds to get your face eaten," Mason said.

Turning around, he slid down the back of the roof and stared up at the empty sky. "What are we going to do?" he asked, but no one seemed to have an answer.

The group sat in silence as Mason's mind raced. He hadn't felt so helpless since he saw Meg reaching from within the scarecrow's ribs.

"Wait a second . . ."

He glanced down at Mr. Crow, who was waiting patiently for them under the roof.

"Mr. Crow," he said, "I have a question for you." The pumpkin head tilted to one side.

"Just how big is that empty space under your jacket?"

CHAPTER 17

A Very Strange Taxi

"Look, I know how it sounds, but hear me out."

They were gathered around Mr. Crow, who knelt, his chest only a foot or so off the ground. His ribs, if you could call them that, had ballooned and opened up, revealing a cavity that was just big enough for two of them to squeeze into, but only if they were *really* close.

"It's not even a full block," Mason added, "and as far as this insane version of Pearl goes, this is like a freaking Uber."

The other three stared from the gaping hole to Mason. It was a look he was used to, one that seemed to say, *You're not right, kid.*

"I guess we could give it a try," Mari ventured.

"Yes," Mason said, "I like the enthusiasm. So, we need to go check on your mom and then get to Mr. Kirby's. We can split up by—"

"I'll go with Serge," Becca volunteered.

"Okay," Mason said, knowing Serge would like that plan. "Mari and I will head to her house, and then Mr. Crow will come back to pick you two up. We'll all meet back up at Mr. Kirby's. We'll get some weapons and then we'll storm the witch's house and get Meg back!"

He was almost surprised at how pumped up he felt, and he had to be careful not to raise his voice too much. They still didn't know where the heart of the spell was, but they finally had a real lead, a real *chance* to get Meg back. That alone was worth getting excited about.

"Okay then," he said. "I'll go first."

From the outside, Mason thought, it looked like a very small tree house, but once he ducked his head in, he found it much more unsettling, like an old bird's nest, long abandoned and empty. He adjusted himself in one corner and looked up at Mari.

"Your turn," he said.

She shuffled forward and stepped into the scarecrow's open frame.

"Okay, if I squeeze in this side . . . I guess I can . . . maybe I should . . ." It was obvious that she wasn't too happy about being crammed into a space the size of a coffin with a boy she barely knew, but there was no getting around it.

"Just go ahead," Mason said finally. "Let's get it over with."

Mari half stepped, half fell into the wooden cavity with a squeaky, creaky drop. Mason took a moment to rearrange himself, pushing as far as he could against one side before Mari joined him. Their legs tangled together like strands of spaghetti, and Mason was suddenly aware of how sweaty he was.

"Okay," Mari said after a moment of shifting around. "That's about as good as it's going to get. Let's go, Mr. Crow."

The ribs creaked and closed in front of them, and in the tight, oppressive darkness, Mason felt as if he had been buried alive. He reached down for something, anything to hold on to as they started to lift off the ground, and in the chaos, Mari placed her hand on top of his. She quickly pulled it away while Mason coughed loudly. He could barely see her face as slices of streetlight peeked through the holes in Mr. Crow's ribs.

"We'll be fine," he said, trying to mask his own nervousness.

"You take a lot of rides inside scarecrows?" she asked.

"It's my first."

Mr. Crow stood up, and Mason could see Becca and Serge through the slats of the scarecrow's ribs.

"You guys make it quick," Becca said.

"We will. Just a quick check-in to make sure she's okay," Mari replied.

"We'll go to Mr. Kirby's house and search for supplies, then we'll send Mr. Crow back to get you," Serge said. "Just keep an eye out for the giant scarecrow."

"He's pretty hard to miss," Mari replied.

Her voice was shaking. Mason might not have admitted it out loud, but he was scared too. He didn't want to leave Serge, and more than that, more than anything, he just wanted this night to be over.

"Hey," Becca said, reaching her fingers between the roots. "I don't know about you, but I'll never think twice about scary movie night again."

Mari laughed, and a tear crept down her cheek as she reached up and held Becca's fingers for a moment.

"We're going to get through this," Mason said.

"Go, Mr. Crow," Mari said suddenly, "before I lose my nerve altogether."

The scarecrow stood to his full height, and they began to bob across the yard, heading toward the light of Orville Avenue. If Mr. Crow was bothered by the extra weight, he made no fuss about it. In a few moments, the sounds of the crowd grew louder, and the streetlights illuminated them. Even though they were well camouflaged, Mari and Mason both pressed back as far as they could to avoid the light. A menagerie of monsters passed by, some mere feet away. They seemed to be growing restless as the long night dragged on, their laughter replaced by growls and shouts. Mari and Mason passed a tall, ratlike creature wearing a metal apparatus on his head with various lights and lenses to help him see. He was wrestling with what looked like a short, hairy potato with stubby arms and legs and a mouth as wide as a bowling ball. The pair was fighting over a piece of brightly colored Halloween candy.

"It's almost gone," the rat man hissed. "This one's mine."

The hairy potato just burped and barked at him, trying to reach up and grab the candy.

Just then, an even taller man with a grisly white face and a black top hat strolled by and snatched the candy from the rat man's hands.

"Thank you kindly." The man popped it into his mouth and began to chew.

"What's so special about that candy?" Mari whispered.

"Yeah, it's weird," Mason said. "You think they could just sneak around and steal candy whenever they wanted." Mr. Scarecrow moved along, and Mason was struck by the feeling that he and Mari were floating in a dangerous sea with nothing to keep them safe but their wooden raft. He reached down and grabbed hold of a tree root as the gruesome faces flew past.

I'll have nightmares for the rest of my life, he thought. All the movies in the world hadn't prepared him for the real thing: the sight of bloody faces, the smell of rotting flesh, and the sounds of gnashing teeth.

"Look," Mari whispered, "it's my building."

On the corner of Orville and Banner, the apartment building loomed like the wall of a redbrick canyon. As Mr. Crow carried them closer, they passed a tall man with a vulture head who stood silently, watching the crowd walk past. A small, wide-eyed monkey sat on his shoulder.

"Aw," Mari whispered. "That one's kinda cute." A moment later, the vulture held up a chunk of raw meat, and the monkey opened its mouth. It was, Mason realized, a snake's mouth, filled with fangs and tiny razor-sharp teeth. The monkey gnawed on the meat, leaving little more than bloody bits on the vulture's black shoulder. Mason gulped, while Mari shuddered beside him. "I take that back," she whispered.

As they approached the building's front door, Mr. Crow leaned down to the stoop and his ribs opened up. Mari stepped out and opened the door before slipping inside. Mason followed close behind her.

"We'll see you in a minute," Mason said, turning back to Mr. Crow.

At least, I hope so.

The scarecrow nodded, and Mason closed the door on his smiling face.

"Wow," he said when he turned around and took in the apartment, but Mari held a finger to her lips.

"We might not be alone," she whispered.

"Yeah, I know, it's just . . . you got a cool house is all."

The building was almost vertical, a series of rooms stacked one on top of the other, and signs of the former business that had occupied it remained. A metal sign that read *Pearl's Finest Dry Cleaning* hung on one wall, half a decoration and half a memory of the past. The unadorned lightbulbs hanging from the ceiling, the brick walls, and the huge industrial sink made it look more like an old workspace than a home. The kitchen was long and narrow, with a metal spiral staircase at the far end winding up to the higher levels. Mason stood awkwardly in the middle of the room as Mari grabbed a few of her mom's bras that were sitting on the countertop and stuffed them into the closest cabinet.

"We weren't expecting company," she whispered.

"It's all good," he said.

They checked the bottom floor, then the second floor, and by the time they reached Mari's room, they realized they were, in fact, alone.

"Wait here while I check the mirror," Mari said as she ran to the bathroom across the hall. From where he stood, Mason could see that the mirror itself took up half the wall, stretching from the vanity to the ceiling. Mari turned this way and that, trying to see anything in that window into their world.

"I don't see anything," she said. "Let me check the other ones." She ran out and disappeared down the stairs, leaving Mason alone in her bedroom.

He immediately felt out of place and awkward, so he tried not to focus too much on any particular personal belonging. There was a small desk, a twin bed, and a TV on top of the dresser. What really caught his eye was the loft built into one corner of the room reached by a short ladder.

"Whoa."

Any thought of respecting Mari's privacy went out the window as Mason climbed up the ladder and sat on the edge of the small landing. There was just enough room for a fat beanbag chair, a scattering of books, and a framed picture of Mari and her parents that sat on the windowsill. From up there, he could see all of Orville Avenue through the broad window as well as the monsters prowling below.

"I thought I told you to wait here," Mari called from the bottom of the ladder.

"You did," Mason confessed, peering down at her, "and I'm sorry, but this place is *amazing*."

Mason's usual nervous energy was cranked up way more than normal, and he suddenly felt a bit guilty about his excitement—they had more important things to focus on after all. He felt relieved when Mari smiled.

"I can't believe this is your room," he said when she climbed up to join him in the loft.

"I guess it's all right," Mari said, pushing the beanbag aside and sitting on the edge next to him. "The view is the best part for sure."

Mason leaned forward, gazing out at the world below.

"It doesn't feel real from up here," he said.

"It never does."

He glanced at the picture of her family, but when Mari saw him looking, Mason quickly cut his eyes away, back to the street below. Even from that quick look, he could see how much she looked like her father. They had the same smile, the same warm brown eyes.

"It's funny watching all those monsters," Mason said. "I never would have thought of it before, but I guess everyone needs a way to get away from everything. Even rat people and weird triplets. Before all this happened, before I knew any better, tonight would have been my dream come true."

"I knew you were a weirdo, but how's this your dream?"

"Well, I don't have a sweet loft to hang out in," Mason said. "Movies work pretty good as a place to get away, though. You watch enough monster movies, you start to root for the bad guys. The misfits. The . . . weirdos."

He caught a tiny glimpse of something in Mari's eyes. Guilt, maybe?

"I can see that," she said a few moments later.

A surprising wave of sadness hit him, and he said, "You know, I've watched so many horror movies, seen so many monsters, so many plots and stupid characters doing the wrong things. You'd think, out of all the things I'm not good at, I'd at least know what to do in a situation like this."

"Don't beat yourself up," Mari said. "There *are* no situations like this."

"I guess so."

They looked back down at the monster-filled street, leaning back once or twice when some black flapping thing flew past the window. *Bat monster*, Mason thought. *That's pretty cool.* The idea of a neat monster immediately changed into the memory of Meg, and he felt even more guilty than he had before.

"I hope we get Meg back," he said. "If we don't . . . I'll never forgive myself."

Mari looked at the picture of her father. For a moment, Mason watched her struggling with what to say next. When she finally spoke, her voice was soft, barely above a whisper.

"That's my dad," she said. "My mom took this picture of us when we went to visit his parents, my grandparents, all the way in Japan." She swallowed hard. "He died three years ago."

For a long while, Mason didn't say anything, and he was afraid that maybe there was nothing he could say.

Finally, he said, "It's hard, isn't it?"

"Yeah."

"I wish it wasn't."

The two of them sat there in silence for a while, gazing down at the street below. From up there, the monsters almost looked like regular old trick-or-treaters.

Almost.

CHAPTER 18

In the Mirror

Mason could hear the steady *thump, thump, thump* of Mari's feet up and down the stairs as she went from room to room checking the mirrors, and he realized that, as cool as it was, there were some clear disadvantages to living in a three-story apartment. He took off his glasses and cleaned them as well as he could on his dirty shirt, then scanned the street below, looking for any sign of the friendly scarecrow.

The crowd was growing rowdier by the minute. What had started as playful and fun was morphing into something brutal and dangerous. The final scraps of Mason's love for monsters had withered away now that he saw the reality. The tall, gaunt man in the top hat walked by once again, swinging an old-timey doctor's bag, and nearly stepped on a squat, bat-like creature. The black bat was probably three feet tall, but it turned and sank its fangs into the man's leg. A moment later, he swung his bag down onto the creature's head, and the two of them stumbled into the shrubs, continuing the fight somewhere unseen.

It was the same on every corner. The transformation from a rowdy Halloween town into a monstrous nightscape was all but complete, and Mason couldn't help but feel the tension rising in him as he watched it all unfold. Just a few short hours ago, the four of them stood at the edge of the woods, watching the monsters walk past, and he had thought his fear couldn't grow any stronger. He tried to remember that he was safer now, locked in an empty house, three stories above the fray. But somehow he felt more vulnerable than ever.

He heard footsteps and turned to see Mari in the doorway. "Any sign of her?"

"No," Mari said, frustrated. "She could be anywhere out there."

"Maybe it's nothing to worry about," Mason said. "If we can find this heart thing . . ."

"What if we can't?" Mari asked. "What if this night ends and she's just . . . gone?"

It was easy for Mason to imagine how she was feeling, because he was feeling the exact same way. From the moment the night began, the deck had been stacked against them. They still had to find a magical heart, save Meg, and find some way out of this place, all while being chased by an all-powerful witch. If he stopped to think about it for long, Mason knew he would want to give up too.

"We can't think like that," he replied. "It won't get us anywhere."

"That's *all* I can think about," Mari said, her lower lip wobbling.

"Well, your mom and my sister are relying on us. Nothing good will come from us just giving up—"

A light suddenly appeared over Mari's shoulder.

A light was glowing from within the bathroom. Mari ran across the hall as Mason scrambled down from the loft. They paused at the threshold of the bathroom and then carefully pushed open the door together.

Like it had in the zombie house, the magic of this place toyed with Mason's brain. Mari's mother was reflected back at them. She still wore her vampire makeup and sleek dress, but her makeup was smudged and her hair was wild and unkempt. To Mason, it looked like the night of partying had taken its toll.

"Mari!" she yelled. "You home? I hope you're home. I can't drive to get you."

Mari's mom giggled and leaned forward against the bathroom sink. Mari and Mason were nowhere to be found in the mirror. Instead, the mirror had become a window into a different reality, a bridge to the world they'd left behind.

"She looks like she had fun tonight." Mason smiled.

"Shut up," Mari snapped, clearly embarrassed.

"Sorry," Mason said. He didn't want to hurt her feelings. "It's Halloween. Grown-ups like to party."

Mari was silent, her gaze never leaving the mirror. They watched for a moment as Mari's mom began to remove her makeup with a washcloth.

"This is kind of weird," Mason said. "I feel like I'm spying on her."

"Well, stop then." Mari pushed him out of the bathroom and shut the door.

Sighing, Mason walked away and glanced back out the window, looking for Mr. Crow. *Where are they?* he wondered. Then, he heard the first growl.

The sound rose up from somewhere beneath his feet, and his first instinct was that one of the monsters had broken through the locked door. But surely he would have heard the sound of breaking glass, so maybe it was a monster that had been hiding somewhere, like the zombies had. Another growl followed, this one lower, more guttural.

"Mari, is that you?" her mom called from behind the locked door.

With a rolling wave of terror, Mason realized the truth. The growl wasn't coming from UnderPearl. Whatever was making the noise was in Pearl, the *real* Pearl, in the house with Mari's mother. He ran to the stairs and raced down, taking them three at a time, looking for a mirror. Mari's mother's room was right at the bottom, and the door was wide open. A full-length mirror hung on the back of the door, and a pair of huge yellow eyes gazed out from it. Mason stumbled back, falling onto the metal stairs hard enough to make him see stars. A sleek creature covered in black fur seemed to stare back at him, and he expected it to leap across the room and tear him to shreds. Instead, the creature didn't seem to notice him at all as it cast its nose upward, sniffing the air.

Werewolf, he thought, and it felt accurate even though the werewolf looked nothing like what Mason had seen in movies. This creature was so tall that it seemed like a performer on stilts. The slick black hair made it look more like a thin, gaunt dog than a wolf, but its face was pure terror, all malice, peeled back lips, and shining teeth.

Mason ran back up the steps and banged on the bathroom door.

"What?" Mari asked, swinging the door open.

"There's a monster in the house," he whispered, then felt foolish. "In your mom's house!"

"Where?"

"On the first floor. I think it's a werewolf!"

"Oh God . . . what do we do?" Mari asked, turning to watch her mom's reflection.

Mason's mind raced back to every werewolf movie he'd ever seen, and he knew there was only one way out of this.

"Do you have anything silver?" he asked.

"What?"

"Like something antique. Like a fork or knife or something."

"I don't know," Mari said, panic rising in her voice.

Her mother turned around and looked out the open door, tilting her head as if she had heard something. She stood in the exact spot that Mari was standing in, but mother and daughter were separated by worlds and magic, a grand illusion that made Mason's head hurt.

"No," Mari said, putting a hand to the mirror, trying to stop the reflection from walking away to her own death. As she touched the mirror, a foggy outline appeared around her fingers, as if she were touching a cold window in the middle of winter.

"Are you home, Mar?" her mother called.

All at once, she turned back around and stared at Mari in the mirror. For a moment, Mason was certain she saw her daughter's face, but there was something else, some leftover bit of magic that maybe the witch didn't intend. Mari pulled her hand away and the impression remained. Her mother's eyes were drawn to it, and she reached forward to touch it.

"She sees it," Mari said. "She sees the outline of my hand."

"Tell her to lock the door," Mason said.

"She can't hear me—"

"Blow on the glass and write it! Tell her she's in danger!"

Mari blew on the mirror, creating a long streak of condensation across the glass. Her mother gasped when it appeared, and Mari began to write with her finger.

Mom, she wrote in small, neat letters, *it's Mari.*

"Mom," her mother repeated, "it's . . . Mari . . ."

Mari was on the verge of tears, but there was no time to stop and think. Mason darted to the stairs and ran halfway down, ducking to see the mirror in the bedroom. The creature was at the base of the stairs now, just a few feet from where Mason stood. It was still sniffing the air, and Mason knew they didn't have long. He ran back upstairs and saw the next line Mari had written.

Lock the door.

"You don't have long," Mason said. "It's right out there! It's coming up the stairs."

As they watched, Mari's mother mouthed the words Mari had written, but she did it so slowly that Mason could hardly stand it. He took a spot on the mirror next to Mari and blew a hard breath onto it.

NOW!

Something about the sharper message, written with a different hand, frightened Mari's mother in a way that almost made Mason feel guilty, but it did the trick. She reached over and slammed the door, locking it behind her as she stared at the bathroom mirror for whatever she needed to do next.

"Mari?" she asked. "What's going on? Are you there?"

Before Mari or Mason could respond, the door on her mother's side of the mirror banged so hard it almost leapt off its hinges. She slammed her body against it.

"Mom!" Mari screamed.

There was nothing they could do to save her. Almost on instinct, Mason leaned close to the mirror, breathed heavily, and began to write furiously.

USE SILVER

Mari's mother squinted and stared, baffled and terrified beyond words. There was no time to think, not for her or for them—a moment later, a clawed hand plunged through the bathroom door as if it were made of tissue paper. Her mother screamed and fell back, her hands rising to the sides of her face as she dropped out of sight behind the bathroom counter.

"Mom!" Mari cried as the bathroom door burst into pieces.

The werewolf, sleek and black and impossibly tall, shoved himself into the bathroom, ripping the remains of the door off its hinges. Splintered bits of wood snapped and flew in all directions. A single, thick piece of the doorframe was launched directly into the mirror, and Mari's mother only had time to scream a single word.

"No!"

The thin window between the two worlds shattered on both sides. Mason and Mari shielded their eyes as countless shards of glass exploded around them. All that remained was an echo of a scream.

CHAPTER 19

Katanas Among Friends

Mari was completely broken. It had been nearly ten minutes since she and Mason saw the awful thing rip into her mother's bathroom and crouch over her, and they had frantically checked the other mirrors in the house, hoping for some sign of what happened. Once, as they peered into the mirror on the ground floor, Mason thought he heard the thump of footsteps, the click of light claws on the wooden floors. *Tink, tink, tink.*

But he saw nothing, and a moment later, the sound was gone.

He's leaving, Mason thought, heart sinking. *The monster did what he was supposed to do, and now he's leaving.*

Mari had gone back up to the bathroom, with Mason following awkwardly. She looked down at the thousand shards spread across the bathroom floor, but it was just mirrored glass now. Whatever spell had been on the mirror was gone. All that was left was her own guilty reflection.

Mari walked calmly into her bedroom and sat on her bed in silence. For a long, stretched-out moment, Mason couldn't quite make himself go any farther than the doorway. All he could do was stare at Mari, who held her head in her hands. She looked older somehow, and in her costume, she reminded him of a real nurse who had just lost a patient, all exhaustion and sadness. He had no idea what to say or do. He'd never felt more useless in his life. He was just a kid in a costume pretending to be a hero from a movie.

"I know it looks bad," he said finally, and walked into the room, "but we have to keep moving. Maybe she made it out, and maybe we can get her some help, but we have to keep going."

Mari said nothing. Mason opened his mouth to speak again but stopped himself.

She's lost them both, he thought. *Mom and dad. And if I can't do something, Meg will be next. It will be me sitting in a room with my head in my hands, crying because I can't do anything to bring her back.*

The realization hit him like a dump truck, and he knew there was nothing left to say. He went over to the window and gazed down just in time to see Mr. Crow walking up the street in their direction.

"Mari," he said softly, "we have to go. Mr. Crow is down there waiting for us."

"She knew," Mari said softly.

Mason took a deep breath. "Look, Mari . . . your mom didn't—"

"Not my mom," she said as she wiped a tear away with her sleeve. "Gloom."

Mason furrowed his brow in confusion. "I don't know what you're talking about."

"The doll," Mari replied. "I've been thinking about it all night. I thought maybe I was just imagining it."

It took Mason a moment, but then he remembered. Just before Gloom vanished, she'd drawn a small doll from her bag. It was only a second, but the details were too similar to be a coincidence. The red dress, the frizzy blond hair, and the vampire makeup.

"She knew all about what was going to happen," Mari said, finally looking up at Mason, her sad eyes filled with fire. "She knew all along."

"But how?" Mason asked. "I mean, I knew she wasn't human, but . . . what is she?"

"She's Death," Mari said, her voice breaking. "That's how she knew."

"Mari, you don't know that. Your mom could have—"

"Could have what?" she demanded. "Fought off a giant wolf monster? She's afraid of spiders. She couldn't have fought off anything!"

"I don't know," Mason said. "But we can't stay here. We have to keep moving or everything that's happened will be for nothing."

"I don't care what else happens." A tear streaked down Mari's cheek.

"You can't give up," he said.

"I'm not," she replied as she wiped her eyes dry. "Gloom

has answers. I'm going to find her and get them. If it kills me, I'm going to get them."

A mask of resolve hardened Mari's face. She marched past Mason, straight down the spiral stairs, and out the front door as he tried to keep up. They found Mr. Crow waiting for them, and they stepped in without a word. Any excitement or fear during their first trip inside the scarecrow was replaced by a stewing silence. Mason didn't know Mari well, but she struck him as the type of person who didn't get angry very often. People like that were tough to rile up, but they were even harder to calm down.

The trip to Mr. Kirby's was without incident except for the giggling clown who loudly honked a horn close enough to make Mason almost scream. A few minutes later, he and Mari felt Mr. Crow lean down, and when the tree roots opened, they found Serge waiting for them in the open doorway of a house Mason never thought he would step inside.

"Quick," Serge said as Mason and Mari slipped through the door. Mason looked over his shoulder and saw Serge pause and lean close to Mr. Crow. "Thanks, man," he whispered. "Hang tight."

Serge held his fist up for a bump, and Mr. Crow looked as confused as a pumpkin-headed scarecrow could look. He held one fist down for Serge to tap gently. The confusion melted into silly glee, and Mr. Crow nodded.

The four friends walked into a bare, utilitarian living room that looked as uncomfortable as any Mason had ever seen. White walls, a gray couch that looked as if no one had ever sat on it, a bookshelf filled with history books. *Yep*, Mason thought. *This is Mr. Kirby's house.*

Becca came around the corner and immediately locked eyes with Mari. "What?" she asked, her brow furrowed. "What happened?"

"I can't talk about it," Mari said. That clearly wasn't good enough for Becca, who grabbed Mari's sleeve and dragged her out of the room. When they were gone, Mason turned and looked at Serge.

"How bad is it?" Serge asked.

"Bad."

Mason told him everything, and when he was done, Serge gave him a blank, helpless look, clearly unsure what to say. After a long pause, he let out a deep breath. "We're running out of time."

"I know," Mason said. "The monsters are getting worse. We're basically defenseless."

"Not necessarily," Serge said. "I was really excited to show you something, but . . . it seems wrong now. I mean, I still need to show you, but it's just . . . not as fun anymore."

"What is it?"

"Follow me."

Serge opened the door to the basement and led Mason down the wooden stairs. The basement's walls were bare white, the floor plain concrete, and it looked like nothing more than a storage space.

"Where is it?" Mason asked.

"There." Serge pointed to the far wall, where racks of

boxes and huge, plastic-top tubs were stacked. Mason walked over and inspected the closest one.

"Ultra Fresh: Long-Lasting Survival Food?" Mason grinned.

"Yeah. There's tons of this stuff in here."

"The rumors are true," Mason said. "Mr. Kirby actually *is* a survivalist."

"Is that really surprising?" Serge asked.

Mason shook his head. "No, not really. But how does this stuff help us?"

"Check door number one," Serge said, pointing at the door tucked between a few shelves.

Mason pushed the door open and flipped a switch on the wall. His jaw dropped.

"Holy crap."

"Exactly."

Axes, swords, guns, and knives hung from the walls, each in their own specific place. Below them, on waist-high cabinets, were countless shelves of ammo, arrows, and who knew what else. It wasn't a room. It was an armory.

"Duuude," Mason breathed, spinning around, not quite believing his eyes. "This is *nuts.*"

"I know, right?"

"Mr. Kirby," Mason said in a hushed, awed tone, "you wonderful lunatic."

"So, here's the real question. What do we do with all this?"

"I'll tell you what we do." Mason pointed to a tactical shotgun on the wall. "We load up a couple of boomsticks, and we go out there and start kicking the crap out of everything that gets in our way."

"Have you ever shot a gun before?" Serge asked.

"Well, no."

"Then we're *not* messing with the guns."

Mason wrinkled his face up, feeling like a kid who expected to eat ice cream for dinner only to find a plate of broccoli.

"We'll take the bow and arrow, then." He reached for a razor-tipped arrow. Serge smacked his hand.

"Have you shot a bow before?"

Mason rolled his eyes and scanned the wall. A shiny blade caught his attention—it was a Japanese sword. A katana. He grabbed the black hilt and turned, his whole body humming with excitement. "Dude."

"Do I have to ask?" Serge said.

Just then, they heard a crash of glass from upstairs. It was hard to say what was happening, but Mason heard three things in the few seconds that followed. Becca screaming uncontrollably. A high-pitched laugh. And, worst of all, a silly, unmistakable honking sound.

"Clown," Serge said as he reached for the nearest weapon, a black machete with a rubber handle. "You really know how to handle that thing?"

"You want to give me a lecture?" Mason asked. "Or do you want to go upstairs and watch me kill a clown with a katana?"

They took the stairs two at a time. Mason knew from a lifetime of watching kung fu movies that sword fighting took a great deal of skill. He wasn't the most graceful person in the world, but holding the sword felt right, as if his entire life had been leading up to this moment. All the doubt and fear were still there, but they had been pushed aside by something stronger.

I got this, he repeated in his head as he topped the stairs and caught a glimpse of the clown in all his terrifying glory.

The white face. The huge red smile. The orange curls. And the huge red nose.

The clown stood in the hall, banging against the closed bedroom door and laughing hysterically.

"Let me *innn,*" he said playfully. "I heard that someone has a *birthday* coming up!"

Mason and Serge both froze when they saw it, but it was Mason who spoke first.

"Hey," Mason said, his voice shaking. He heard a voice in his head, very faint and tiny, begging him to turn and run, to drop the sword and stop pretending to be the hero. Mason told that voice to *shut up* as he drew the blade.

The clown turned slowly, his grin widening impossibly far. His lips peeled back, revealing teeth that looked like yellowing chips of stone. He reached up and grabbed his nose, giving it a loud *honk* that reverberated off the walls.

What happened next was a blur. Something about holding that sword seemed to awaken a sleeping power inside of Mason, and he dashed forward, closing the gap between him and the clown in a few steps. He leapt and swung the sword, which actually whistled as he floated past the clown.

The blade was almost unthinkably sharp. All Mason had to do was aim it.

Mason never looked back as he stood, sword outstretched, a hero waiting for the inevitable sound of his enemy falling. There was a tumbling sound, and Mason saw the curly red head lying on the ground. The headless body reached down and snatched up the painted head, then held it aloft for Mason to see.

"*No fair!*" the clown screamed before running past Mason, laughing hysterically and honking his red nose as he vanished out the front door and into the night. Mason shut the door and glanced back at his friends. For the first time since the night started, he felt like he was no longer wearing a costume.

He looked down at his sword, then up at Serge. He couldn't remember a moment in his life when he had felt so triumphant. *Is this what Serge feels like all the time?* he wondered.

"Did that just happen?" he asked quietly.

The girls walked out of the bedroom and stopped behind Serge. All three gazed at Mason, amazed at what they had just witnessed.

This is it, Mason thought as he pushed up his glasses. *Say something cool.*

"Looks like . . . the circus is closed. Or, wait . . . the circus has left town. Yeah, the second one."

Mari let out a snort, followed by a choked laugh. It must have been the stress getting to her. With everything that had happened—her mom, the town, all of it—it seemed

177

impossible that Mari would actually laugh. But once she started, she seemed powerless to stop.

"Is she okay?" Mason asked Becca, but he got no answer. She was still terrified and could only stare at the front door, as if she expected the clown to burst back inside.

"The circus *left town*?" Mari gasped, trying not to cry. She suddenly leaned forward and wrapped her arms around Mason, laughing and crying into his shoulder.

"Oh my goodness," she said. "Thank you. I needed that."

Mason glanced at Serge and Becca. They just shrugged and smiled weakly.

"No problem," Mason said.

Once Mari had calmed down, she and Becca went into the basement to grab their own weapons while Serge and Mason watched the front door. A few minutes later, the girls returned. Becca still had the baseball bat and Mari had settled for a heavy crowbar.

"I can't believe it," Mason said, a renewed sense of purpose buzzing through him, "but this might actually work."

With the finish line closer than ever, all he could think about was Meg. She was alone—no, worse than alone. She was with a witch who intended to do something awful to her.

"We finally have a shot at getting Meg back. A *real* shot. We got some weapons, and we can follow Mr. Crow to the witch's house. I don't know what we're going to find in there, but I'm ready. Whatever it takes, I'm going to try. Are you guys ready?"

"As ready as we're going to be," Mari said.

"Let's finish this thing," Becca added.

Mason looked from the girls to Serge.

"Let's go get Meg," Serge said.

Mr. Crow's face brightened—literally—his eyes flaring with green flames when the four friends poked their heads out the door.

"Big man," Serge whispered, "is the coast clear?"

The pumpkin head nodded, and Mason ushered the group onto the porch.

"Are you okay leading the way?" Mason asked, and the friendly scarecrow nodded again, clearly pleased to be part of the team. He led the way through the dark backyards, east on Orville Avenue, toward the witch's house. Thankfully, the monster party was still raging in the street, and the backyards remained deserted.

It took them ten minutes before they came to an older house that, from behind at least, was lightly decorated by Pearl standards. Mr. Crow hid behind a hedge, and the others joined him. His green flames flickered and dimmed a bit, and Mason realized that the scarecrow was afraid.

"Is this it?" Mason asked.

The scarecrow nodded. Mason looked at the house again, and some of the fog in his brain lifted a bit. He could practically see it all unfolding in his mind. *Meg was right there,* he thought. *And that witch was on the porch . . . just waiting.* He curled his hands into fists.

"All right," he said through gritted teeth, "it's time to end this. We need to get the witch out of the house and down the street a little. I'm thinking we can . . . can . . ."

"What?" Mari asked, then added, "Wait . . . there's . . . something . . ."

Mason turned toward the others. His vision blurred for a moment, and it felt like his brain was . . . itching. There was a crackling sound, like someone turning an old radio dial in search of a station. Then the static cleared and he heard it. He looked at the others again, and by their wide eyes and terrified expressions, they were all experiencing the same thing.

"What is that?" Serge asked, holding a hand to the side of his head.

Mason closed his eyes and listened. Somehow, a voice was speaking directly into his mind.

"It's the witch," he said as she continued to speak.

CHAPTER 20

It Doesn't Hurt at All

Meg let her eyes drift shut. It was the only thing she could do. She'd been sitting in the witch's chair for what felt like weeks, though she knew that wasn't possible. She would have starved to death by now. Even so, time no longer made any sense, and every second seemed to stretch out like a piece of taffy folding over itself, on and on without end.

The sensation of being bitten by invisible teeth had thankfully ended, but the strangeness was still there, all around her. When Meg finally opened her eyes again, the swirling shape above her was melting down the walls, coating it like candle wax. The details of the room, the strange objects, the tiny jars, the moldering books, became smooth and shapeless as the colors ran down to the floor. The entire room had become a swirling vortex of orange and black, and she floated in the center. Somehow, she felt even more woozy and off-kilter, and once again it felt as though she were being drawn upward, pulled by invisible threads, detached from herself. She closed her eyes. She wasn't Meg at all—she was something tiny, something wrapped, something that existed in a world of crystal.

She was something good to eat.

Was she crying? When had that started, and how had she not known it before now?

It's because there's hardly anything left of you, she thought. *It's because they've almost eaten you up.*

It couldn't be true. She was still *there,* still attached to the chair. She could feel it if she really concentrated, could feel the leather straps biting into her wrists, could feel the chill of the basement, the rough texture of the wood. She was still Meg, still just a girl tied to a chair.

That's your body, she thought.

She had always thought her body was what mattered. When she fell and skinned her knee or dropped something on her foot, the pain was the most real thing in the entire world. Her physical self was all that had mattered before now.

The truth was so much more than she could handle.

It would hurt if they ate your body, she thought. *But this . . . it doesn't hurt at all, and that makes it worse. Somehow, it's a thousand times worse.*

She opened her eyes again. The room was completely wrapped in the swirling vortex. It had curled up under her feet, and she realized as it touched her plastic princess shoes that it was a thick, living liquid. It was climbing the chair now, and she tried to pick her feet up to get away, but she was too weak and tired. A slow, pulsing warmth inched up her legs, wrapping her up like a blanket fresh from the dryer.

This is it.

CHAPTER 21

The Red Witch of Pearl

The bowl was filled once more, but Serpa Vernon, the Red Witch of Pearl, knew that the spell was almost complete. The girl was nearly spent, and her monsters were restless, as they always were once the night was over. All the same, she was pleased she had given them a night they would remember. Most would return next year, bringing her gifts and presents, potions and spices, gold and ancient scrolls with forgotten spells. A few of the creatures that could pass for human would carry the treasures to her home in the real world, and she would wait for the following year to come. It was a fine life she had made for herself, but she had plans, dark and secret. The monsters adored her, but the truth was all this work wasn't for them. Serpa simply enjoyed watching children vanish into thin air. For all the work and effort she had put into Pearl, it was just one town, one little hive of children.

The dream she kept in the back of her mind was so much more *ambitious*.

One perfect spell.

Serpa pictured it, felt herself giving it life, and saw the thousands—no, *millions*—of parents waking up to find their children's beds filled with perfectly wrapped pieces of candy. Oh, it would be like Christmas morning.

Unfortunately, those dreams would have to wait. Her wolf hadn't returned yet, but she had little cause for worry. He was, after all, likely wild from his hunt. She might not see him for weeks as he stalked across the hills at night, feasting on whatever creatures were foolish enough to cross his path. Even so, Serpa realized that while he might do well as an assassin, the wolf was not a proper minion.

Yes, those children were still out there, but the chances were very high that they were already dead. There were too many monsters with too many hungry mouths for them to survive the night. She could send another crow out to track them, but why bother? None of it would matter in a few short hours. The ritual was almost complete. She would lead the monsters out of UnderPearl, and once she did, she'd take the heart and end the spell for another year. The town would disappear, and anyone, monster or human, that stayed behind would be gone as well. Next year, she would use the heart to make a new copy of the town, and the ritual would start anew.

She pictured the heart and smiled. It was, without question, her greatest creation, a delicate, multifaceted stone as complex as any computer chip. With that stone, she could bend reality to her will, and the people of Pearl would forever be under her sway—as long as it was kept safe.

What might happen to anyone who was left inside when the spell ended? There was no way to know for sure. Even witches as powerful as she was didn't know all the great mysteries. Perhaps they would blink out of existence completely. Or drift into an endless void, stuck between worlds for all eternity, never dying or truly living. Perhaps their minds would break, their senses dull, and each moment would become longer than the one before.

"Ooh," Serpa said with a grin. "I need to write that down."

She placed the bowl back on its pedestal and covered it once more. A moment later, she pulled the cover off and looked inside.

A single piece of candy remained.

"And one for me," she said with a laugh.

Usually she liked to save her piece for the next day, once all the chaos had died down and she could enjoy it in peace, but this had been a stressful night.

"Oh, what will it hurt?"

She unwrapped the candy and held it between her fingers. The artistry of the spell was impeccable. The candy was a perfect disk of solid black with delicate swirls of orange and gold. The pinwheels of color seemed to spin as she twisted the candy in the light, admiring her work. Then she placed it on her tongue and closed her eyes as it dissolved.

"Mmm . . . divine."

The beginning of the end was at hand. She threw her cloak back on and picked up her grinning cane. "Come now,

Henry," she said as she walked out into the street. They'd worked themselves into a frenzy at this point, her monsters, foaming and fighting as their night of mayhem came to its wild conclusion. Serpa walked into the center of the street and whispered a quick spell. When she spoke a moment later, her voice was low and clear, and every single creature in the town heard it as if she were standing just inches away, speaking into their ears.

"My dear friends, I hope you have enjoyed this night, made just for you," she said.

The snarling, slavering beasts all around her were suddenly silenced. Monsters that had been in the middle of ripping each other to pieces froze.

That's right, she thought. *Your master is speaking.*

"As always, we must say our goodbyes. The door will close soon. We will meet at the fountain in one hour. Don't be late.

"But before we leave," she added dramatically, "let us have one more moment that is ours. One more chance to remind ourselves of what *we* are. Monsters, friends, it's time."

Serpa raised the cane, closed her eyes, and began to recite the spell. She heard the jack-o-lanterns on the porches and sidewalks begin to vibrate and hum. Without opening her eyes, she knew trickles of blood were weeping from their mouths and eyes. Up and down Orville, the spell carried like a dark wind, and when she finally opened her eyes, dozens of monsters were staring at her in anticipation, waiting for her word to begin.

"Paint this street *red*!"

Howls rang up and down the street, bloodcurdling shrieks

that would scourge the soul of the bravest men and women. A wild horde of monsters ran to the nearest pumpkins, snatching them up and rushing back to the center of the street with their sloshing prizes. The town's residents had never considered where the tradition of smashing pumpkins came from. Little did they know, their custom was only an echo, a faint mirror of a much darker ritual led by the true master of the town. The Red Witch of Pearl raised her head and laughed defiantly at the sky as the pumpkins were smashed, raining down on the pavement, covering the street with gallons of fresh blood. Soon, the streets were soaked red as the gutters choked on bloody pumpkin guts.

One hour, she thought as she gazed lovingly at the blood-soaked streets. *One more chance for monsters to be monsters.*

CHAPTER 22

An Empty Chair

As terrifying as it was to feel like someone was whispering in his brain, Mason realized it was just the appetizer. The main course followed soon after as the horde of monsters smashed hundreds of bloody pumpkins in the street.

"This is *wild*," Becca said.

They were still ducked down behind the bushes outside the witch's house, and none of them wanted to venture out after what they had just witnessed.

"One hour," Mari whispered.

"We're running out of time," Mason replied with a swell of panic. "What are we going to do?"

"Look," Serge said, pointing at the street. They could see, in the gap between the bushes, a line of monsters walking slowly up the street. At the head of the procession strode the Red Witch.

"It's her," Mason said, standing up, clutching his katana.

"Sit your butt down," Mari hissed. "Let them get out of the way first."

"We could take her," Mason said to Serge. "We could just run up there and lop her head off."

"You got lucky with the clown," Mari said. "You'd get torn apart by all those monsters."

"And besides," Serge said, "the house should be empty. We don't even need the distraction now."

"Yeah, let's go get Meg first," Becca said. "You remember Meg, right? Your *sister*?"

Mason didn't like Becca's tone, but he knew she was right. They were here for a reason. Besides, actually taking out the witch might not even be possible, especially for a kid with a sword that he barely knew how to use.

"All right," Mason said, his voice shaking. "Let's go in."

The four kids and the scarecrow walked through the backyard and onto the small concrete deck. Serge tried the door—unlocked—and they quietly snuck inside.

"Can you squeeze in?" Serge asked Mr. Crow, who was still on the porch.

The scarecrow folded himself into a crouch and slipped through the doorway. Serge patted him on the shoulder as he made his way inside. The scarecrow's smile deepened as he scuttled past Serge.

He's getting attached, Mason thought, heart sinking. *I hope this turns out okay . . . for all of us.*

"All right," Mason said, his heart pounding. "Where is she?"

The entire night had been leading to this moment, and now that they were actually in the witch's house, it all felt surreal and impossible. The home was a little odd by most standards, but there were no stretched skins drying on the walls, no furniture made of bones, no broomsticks in the corner.

Of course not, Mason thought. *She's got to blend in.*

"Come on," he said, turning to Mr. Crow. "Where would the witch put her?"

Mr. Crow squeezed past the kids and led them out of the small living room and down a hallway. The house was tiny but well kept, and as they passed the kitchen, Mason poked his head in. The room smelled of heavy spices, and he thought of apple pie and hot cider.

"Not what I expected," Mari said as she poked her head in next to him.

"No cauldrons, huh?"

She rolled her eyes. "Let's keep moving."

The hallway was painted a deep red and the floors were dark wood. It felt a bit like they were inside an artery or a vein, as if the house was alive somehow. Mr. Crow stopped halfway down the hall and pointed at a closed door.

"Meg's in there?" Serge asked.

Mr. Crow nodded and pointed downward.

"The basement?" Mason asked, and Mr. Crow nodded once more.

Mason opened the door and turned on the light. Unlike Mr. Kirby's basement, this one was finished. The stairs were the same polished wood as the hallway, and an unfamiliar scent drifted up to greet them.

"I . . . I guess I'll go first," Mason said cautiously. It wasn't fear he felt in that moment, at least not fear of a monster he might have to fight. This was a deeper terror, something almost primal, a fear made stronger by love. He knew full well that he might find his sister dead in that basement, and the knowledge froze him in place.

"I can go first," Serge said.

"No," Mason said. "It should be me."

Mr. Crow waited as the kids walked down the rickety stairs single file. The walls were covered with thick red and purple drapes.

"This is a witch's lair," Mason said.

The air was heavy with something he couldn't place. Like the way the air smelled before a thunderstorm, only sweeter.

"It smells so weird," Becca said, as if reading his mind.

"Yeah," Mari agreed as they reached the bottom of the stairs. "It's like . . . electric vanilla, if that makes sense."

Knickknacks lined the tables and shelves—jars full of pickled animals and tiny limbs, herbs and crystals, ingredients for charms and spells—but one thing stood out. An electric chair sat in the middle of the room. The shackles on its arms and legs were still locked, but they were ominously empty. In the center of the chair was a small, handmade doll of a girl in a light-blue dress. There was no mistaking the likeness.

"Where is she?" Mason said. *"Where is she?"*

"Gone," a voice said from a corner. Gloom stepped out of the shadows, and for the first time, she wasn't smiling. Mari took a step forward, and Mason could see her knuckles turning white as she gripped the crowbar.

"You knew," Mari said. "You knew about all of this. You knew about my mom!"

"The future is impossible to know," Gloom said softly as she picked up the doll and held it by one stubby arm. "The dolls are as close to being a fortune-teller as I can get. They show up whenever someone is . . . close to meeting me. It's like getting a notification on your phone that your table is ready at a restaurant."

Mari looked at Mason, and he got the feeling that she expected him to back her up, for the two of them to team up in their rage. But at that moment, he simply didn't have it in him. At the sight of the empty electric chair and the tiny doll, all his fire had gone out.

Meg is gone, he thought, the idea echoing inside the hole in his heart. For the first time that night, he felt like exactly what he was. They were all just kids, in way over their heads, and he was a big brother without a little sister.

"What happened to her?" he asked.

"What always happens. The spell is slow. I don't think it's painful, at least not for her body. She's . . . removed from herself, so to speak. Separated. That smell in the air, that *electric vanilla*? It's her. It's the memory of the part of her that matters."

"Her soul," Mason said.

"Yes."

There was no sugarcoating it, no more riddles. Just the truth, however painful.

"Why?" Mason asked, not sure whether he really wanted to hear the answer.

"It's Halloween," Gloom said, "and everyone wants a treat.

193

Even monsters. In this room, the witch carried out her cruel-est spell. Your sister's soul was extracted, turned into treats for the monsters, and handed out as candy. To them, nothing is sweeter than a child's soul."

A heavy silence fell over the room as the truth was finally made clear. Mason tried not to notice that the others were looking at him, waiting to see his reaction.

"So, it's over?" he asked as the sword slipped from his hand. "She's gone?"

"Yes . . . and no," Gloom said. "As long as a single piece of that candy hasn't been eaten, she exists somewhere else. Somewhere *between*."

"There's nothing you can do?" Mari asked.

Gloom sighed wearily, and Mason pictured the young girl as an exhausted retail worker nearing the end of her shift. "There's a way to bring her back."

Mason wiped his running nose. "There is?"

"Yes."

"No tricks? No riddles?"

Gloom sighed again, seeming more human than ever be-fore. "My job isn't . . . easy, but it's always harder when it comes to children. Death is a fact of life. Every link in the great chain of humanity has a beginning and an end. People kill each other every single day, and I can't step in and stop it. And yet . . . what's happening here, in this small town, is beyond mere cruelty. The Red Witch has locked the souls of these children away from where they should be. I'm not sup-posed to pick sides, but I want to see this spell ended for good so that all of these children can rest in peace."

Mason thought of Marco, and his heart ached. Marco was dead, as Mason had always feared, yet somehow it was even worse than that. His soul was lost as well.

"It's too late for the others," Gloom said. "But there's still a chance for Meg. That single piece of candy is like a thread keeping a ship from drifting out to sea. You get me one of those pieces, and I'll bring your sister back."

"Okay," Mason said, picking the sword back up, a frantic kind of hope spreading through him. "We need to find some candy, we need to find that heart, and . . . somehow . . . we need to take out the witch once and for all."

"Wait," Mari said, "think about what the witch said. She told the other monsters to meet at the fountain in Pearl Park."

"Holy crap!" Mason said, jumping up and down. "The fountain is the exit!"

"You're smart kids," Gloom said. "I knew you'd get there eventually. Like I said, the heart radiates magic. The center of town is a perfect place for her to hide it. Very convenient for her to grab it on the way out."

"Wait," Mari said. "What about my mother?"

Gloom's smile returned.

"Don't smile at me," Mari snapped. "Is she okay?"

"Now we're getting back into, let's say, *usual* territory. I'm afraid I can't interfere more than I already have."

"What? You knew it was going to happen!"

"Now, now, I *never* know what's going to happen. But I often see what's likely to happen. The rest was up to you."

"That's not good enough!"

Mari marched across the room, crowbar raised. Mason gulped. She meant to use it.

"You're going to tell me what I need to know, or—"

Gloom's laugh cut her off, and in that slight sound echoed something great and hollow, like bones rattling at the bottom of a very deep well.

"Or what?" Gloom said, stepping back into the darkness that she had come from. A soft wind blew through the windowless room, and a black shadow crept across the ceiling. All that was left was a mocking voice, echoing:

"Or what . . . ?"

Mari screamed and slammed the crowbar into the electric chair once, twice, a third time. By the time she stopped, panting, the chair was split in two.

"There's nothing left I can do," she sobbed. "I might as well just sit down here and wait for this whole place to disappear. . . ."

Becca crept forward and wrapped her best friend in her arms, burying her in a tangle of blond curls. Mari didn't fight it, just sank into her. After a moment, Serge stepped forward and hugged them both.

Mason was still scared, still not sure what to do, but then he took a breath and joined them, and the four of them hugged, silent except for the occasional sniffle.

There was a creaking sound, and suddenly their little group was lifted up off the ground. Mason opened his eyes and saw the grinning face of Mr. Crow.

I bet he's never had a hug before, Mason thought. A few

short hours ago, being hugged by a scarecrow was just about the furthest thing in the world from his mind.

When they finally separated, Mari wiped her eyes. "Thank you," she said softly.

"I'm sorry," Becca said. "We all are."

"I'm still scared," Mari said. "Scared for my mom. Scared for me. But at least I'm not doing this alone."

Mason smiled at her and then sighed deeply, steeling himself for what they'd soon be facing.

CHAPTER 23

A Serious Distraction

"Okay, let's lay all this out and come up with a plan," Mason said. They were back upstairs in the witch's den. No one wanted to sit on her couch, but Mason was too tired to care. Serge, still nervous about all that had happened, lingered by the front door, occasionally peeking out the window.

"Have any of the plans actually worked?" Serge asked.

Becca laughed, and Mason glanced over at her. She had her back to the group and appeared to be absorbed in the old black-and-white pictures of the town that lined the walls. She flipped open a rolltop desk, studying the weird contents inside: a feather pen and an inkwell, some rolls of yellowed paper. Along the back of the desk stood a row of small bottles capped with corks. The labels had little hand-painted icons— skulls and crossbones, big red drops of blood, and cartoon frogs or lizards.

"All right, we know the monsters are in the square, and we know we need to find one piece of candy to get Meg back," Mason said, turning back to Mari and Serge.

"Right," Mari replied.

"But we still don't know where, or what, this spell's heart is. Without that, we have no chance of defeating the witch for—"

"You ever see one of these?" Becca interrupted, holding out her hand.

In her palm was a stone the size of a large coin. It looked like a hunk of purple rock candy.

"Um, no," Mason answered.

"It's an amethyst. And this," she said, holding out her other hand, "is a bloodstone. And here's an amber. And a striped carnelian. But *this* . . . is an alexandrite. It's super rare."

"Okay," Mason said, not sure where she was going with this.

"I was kinda obsessed with gems for a while," Becca said. "Looks like the witch is too."

"Maybe it's just a witch thing," Serge said. "Maybe she uses them for spells."

"Exactly!" Becca exclaimed. "Gloom said it was something small, right? Something easy to hide? What if it's a gem?"

"Okay," Mason said, "A good guess, but where would she hide it?"

"Wait." Mari leaned forward. "We know that all the monsters are going to the middle of town, where they'll exit through the fountain, and that the witch is ending the spell in . . . half an hour."

"Okay . . . okay . . . okay . . . ," Mason said, his head spinning. "We've got to find a way into Pearl Park so we can look for the heart."

"We can't just go waltzing through the town square and start looking around," Serge said. "We'd be dead in like two seconds."

"I know that," Mason said, frustrated. "I . . . don't know what to do."

"Oh my gosh," Becca said suddenly. "The naked butt guy!"

They looked at her as if a bird had laid an egg on top of her head.

"What?" Mari asked.

"The naked butt guy!" Becca repeated, pointing at one of the black-and-white framed prints on the wall. The others stood and joined her, and Mason saw what looked like a time line of Pearl as it grew from a small horse-and-buggy town to what it was today. The last picture showed the statue of Bacchus being installed.

"The drunko dude." Becca tapped the frame. "Mr. Wine God, or whatever."

"What in the *heck* are you talking about?" Mason asked.

She ripped the picture off the wall and held it out.

"The statue in the fountain! He's holding up a big cup, right? Perfect place to hide one of these!"

She opened her hand, the gemstones glinting in the dim light.

Mari looked from the stone to the picture and back again.

"Gotta admit, it's a pretty good place to hide something,"

she said. "That statue is taller than it looks. I'd hate to climb up there."

"It's all in here," Becca said, pointing to the desk. "I bet this is where she does her work. Her planning. Look at all this stuff. And I'd bet money that she's got something like this hiding in that cup!"

Mason plucked one of the stones from her palm. It was the striped carnelian, a smooth piece of stone streaked with red and orange.

"I bet you're right," he said, the pieces falling into place. "The exit's the fountain and the heart's a gem. It's got to be there.

"The real question," he continued, "is how do we get it out. The monsters are crowding around the fountain as we speak. There's no way we can get in there without some kind of distraction. Plus . . . without the candy, we'll never get Meg back."

Once again, Mason felt the enormity of the situation weighing on him. Mari put a hand on his shoulder, but before anyone could say a word to comfort him, Serge spoke from across the room.

"Guys?" He had pulled back the curtain and was peering out the window at the empty, blood-soaked street. "Look."

They crowded around the window. The streets were deserted except for a familiar silhouette. The triplets were still holding hands and walking as if they didn't have a care in the world.

"That," Serge said, "might just be our distraction." Then

he pointed at the neat, tiny bag that dangled from one of the triplet's hands.

"And *there* is your candy."

Out of all the terrible plans that they had pulled together, this was unquestionably the worst. Serge had listened considerately, but Mason could see how much he hated the idea. Now that the two of them stood at the edge of the porch, Mason was pretty sure he hated it himself. This night had driven them to wild places that none of them could have expected, and he was beginning to wonder how much more they could take.

"We can do this," Mason said. "I trust you."

"It's not your trust I'm worried about," Serge said.

"Look, you're the fastest one by far. And you *never* get tired."

"I get tired," Serge said. "And I'm hungry. That'll probably slow me down."

"I'll be out there with you," Mason said.

"We don't even know what those things can do. . . ."

"Yeah, but it's got to be awful," Mason replied, forcing himself to sound upbeat. Serge looked appropriately terrified.

"What I mean is, they'll make a good distraction. We get them wound up, they do . . . whatever it is they do, and all the monsters turn away long enough for Mari and Becca to grab the gem from the fountain. You'll be able to outrun those tiny little legs *easy*. Plus, I'll watch your back, and if you get into trouble, I'll sword their little butts. Easy."

"Easy."

"Easy . . ."

"What if it doesn't work?"

"Then we try something else," Mason said. "And besides, we got the big guy with us!"

He pointed at Mr. Crow, who was nervously folding his hands across his chest.

"We can handle the little guys, right, Mr. Crow?"

The corners of the scarecrow's eyes drooped, and he slowly shook his head.

"You're not filling me with confidence," Serge said. "If he's scared of them, that can't be a good sign."

Mason tried to push the fear he was feeling out of his mind. He had to be there for Serge. Mari and Becca emerged from the house. "We're going for the heart," Mari said.

"So, you guys better do a good job," Becca said. "Otherwise, by the time you get there, the witch will turn us into frogs or something."

Serge laughed nervously. "I wouldn't want that."

"You ready?" Mason asked him.

Serge shook his head. "I always feel a little sick before a football game. All those lights just kind of get to me. But now . . . I just feel . . . scared."

"You might not realize it," Mason said, "but Meg's your little sister too."

"All right then." Serge cleared his throat. "Let's do it for Meg."

Mari stood between them and wrapped her arms around both boys at the same time.

"Watch out for each other," she said.

"We'll see you in the middle of town," Serge said as the group broke apart. "Just keep an eye out for the little monsters chasing us."

"Stay out of sight and move slow," Mason told the girls. "There's plenty of places to hide on the way to the square." They left the porch and split up, with Mr. Crow staying with the boys. Mason and Serge went left after the triplets, who were slowly walking west on Orville. Becca and Mari started north toward the square. Mason glanced back once and saw Mari was too. They gave each other a quick wave, and a few moments later, the girls disappeared from sight.

"We got this," Serge said.

Mason glanced over at Mr. Crow. "Confidence, right, Mr. Crow?" The pumpkin head turned and looked at him nervously. "I really wish you could talk and tell us what we're in for."

The scarecrow knew what the triplets were, and he was terrified. And despite his brave words to Serge, that was enough for Mason to be terrified too.

The little trio was a few blocks down the street now, but it didn't take long for the boys to catch up.

Mason drew his sword and motioned to Mr. Crow. They slunk down behind a picket fence, and after a few seconds, a brambly hand stuck up and gave Serge a thumbs-up.

The triplets walked in unison, like windup dolls. Serge kept a steady pace behind them, staying in the shadows. Mason and Mr. Crow followed, running through yards along the row of fences, staying close in case they were needed.

After a few seconds of sneaking along, Mason realized that their attempts at stealth really didn't matter.

The triplets didn't seem to notice anything around them. When they hit the corner, they turned sharply, still in sync, their tiny legs shuffling tirelessly. Serge glanced back as he followed them, and Mason poked his head up over the fence.

"They're getting close to the square," he whispered loudly. "Get their attention."

"How?"

Mason looked around, then pointed to a small flower bed a few feet from Serge.

"The gravel," Mason said. "Throw it at them."

Serge grabbed a handful, then picked up his pace to close the distance. He tossed a piece of gravel the size of a bean. It soared through the air, almost as if in slow motion, before plunking off the head of the creature in the middle. Serge and Mason both held their breath as they waited for something horrible to happen, but the trio just kept pattering along. Serge threw another, larger rock, this time quite a bit harder. It hit the one on the right in the shoulder. The blow was hard enough that Mason knew the creature *had* to feel it. Again, the triplets kept walking.

"It's not working," Serge whispered. Mason threw up his hands in frustration. He scanned the yard and found a smooth oblong rock the size of a baseball. He snatched it up and leapt over the fence and into the road.

"Here," Mason whispered.

"What do you want me to do, give them a concussion?" Serge whispered back.

"We have to get them to follow us to the square," Mason said. "Don't overthink it, just throw it."

Serge cocked his arm, hopped forward, and launched the stone like a rocket. It whizzed through the air and hit the middle creature square in the back. The three continued on as if nothing had happened.

"Oh, forget this," Serge said. Before Mason could stop him, Serge dashed up the street and stood in front of the triplets. They walked slowly toward him, making no sign that they noticed him at all.

"Stop!" he called, holding his hand up. "I . . . uh . . . halt!"

They continued heading directly toward him, and he had to jog backward to keep from being run over. They were still holding hands, the one on the left clutching the tiny bag that rustled as they walked. Mason, who had jumped back over the fence and was keeping pace from yard to yard, poked his head up from behind an inflatable coffin. Mr. Crow, who was mimicking his movements, stuck his head up as well. "Did you think that would work?" Mason asked.

"You come up with something!" Serge yelled back.

Mason emerged from hiding and ran in front of the creatures. "Hey, stop walking."

Again, the triplets made no sign of seeing him.

"I'm talking to you. . . ."

He reached down and slapped the little bag out of the creature's hand.

The pattering feet stopped, and all three heads snapped mechanically toward Mason.

"Dude, why are they looking at me?"

"You wanted a distraction . . . ," Serge said, his voice trailing off. The boys began to back away, and for a moment, the monsters didn't move. Then the one on the right reached into its miniature jacket and retrieved something small and shiny.

"Are those . . . scissors?" Serge asked. "Oh, crap."

Mason looked down at the bag, which had spilled onto the ground. The contents shined like little gems on the dull concrete. Three pieces of candy perfectly wrapped in black-and-orange paper.

The candy.

He knew what he needed to do, what he *had* to do for Meg. But he simply could not move, at least not until he saw what the scissors were for.

The creature's small hand rose, bringing the scissors up to its mouth. Heavy stitches were punched through the lips, sealing them shut, and the little hand went to work, nimbly cutting them free. It took only a few seconds, and then the triplet handed the scissors off to his brother, who promptly did the same. If there were eyes in those grim little faces, Mason never saw them, only those jagged, too-big mouths. They looked like pieces of burlap that someone had ripped open with their bare hands.

"What . . . is . . . happening?" Mason whispered, but Serge shot him a helpless look. They were witnessing something awful, something that was impossibly *new* in this endless night of horrors.

Serge somehow found the nerve to run forward and go

for the candy. The closest of the triplets whipped its head around and looked at him, and the simple act of being *noticed* was enough to make Serge stumble.

That's it, Mason thought, *he's dead.*

But Serge was able to regain his footing and reach down, grabbing a single piece of candy before backing quickly away. Mason felt a sense of relief like he'd never felt in his life before as he and Serge turned and ran up the street, away from the still-unmoving triplets.

"Thank you," he said breathlessly.

"Thank me when we get Meg back. Now, about that—"

Serge glanced back over his shoulder—and froze.

Mason spun around. Something very strange was happening in the street behind them.

Almost a full block separated the triplets and the boys, but Mason had never felt smaller, which was odd considering how small the triplets were. The creatures stood for a short moment with their mouths unstitched, and then the one in the center slipped the scissors back into his tiny jacket. The triplets stared at Mason and Serge, their mouths gaping open. Mason expected to see teeth hiding behind those stitches, but instead he saw nothing at all. It wasn't just darkness; it was something deeper, impossible for light to pierce, like a shimmering pool of black ink. The three creatures locked hands again, looking like schoolchildren on their way home after a long day. Then, as one, they tilted their heads up toward the sky.

Their mouths stretched open even wider, and from where he stood, Mason could see something white stirring inside that deep, infinite blackness. Something was coming out, and when it began to emerge, Mason understood, in a horrible moment of clarity, that these three little monsters were not really monsters at all. They were *doorways,* portals that had been hastily stitched shut to keep whatever vast, unthinkable horror that lurked within them locked in place. In that moment, he understood why the other monsters steered clear of these abominations.

"Serge . . ."

"Mason . . ."

As the two of them stood frozen, the true monster emerged. On each side of the yawning mouths, fingers reached out, long and ghostly pale, followed by thin, reedy arms and then knobby elbows. The arms stretched, popping and cracking, and then the hands reached down to the ground, lifting the triplets high into the air like an awful spider. The creatures were little more than puppets now, empty husks devoid of all life that still managed to hold hands, to link together as one.

The mouth in the center stretched even wider, and the last thing Mason saw before Serge grabbed his shoulder and pulled him away was the face hiding *inside* the mouth. The triplets might have been eyeless, but this face had eyes, merciless, unfeeling yellow orbs that shined out of a ghastly white face. It seemed much too big to squeeze through the tiny mouth, but through sheer will, the creature pushed through, emerging into the world like a butterfly from a cocoon.

The dimensions were confusing, impossible, *wrong.* The head stretched forward on the end of a long dinosaur neck, and it snapped at the air with a mouth full of teeth like those of a deep-sea fish. It was, quite simply, the most alien thing Mason had ever seen.

Because that's what it is, he thought as he tried to run, his legs feeling like jelly. *It's not supposed to be here.*

The yellow eyes locked on the two boys like spotlights, and the world slowed to a crawl. Mason felt as if he were in a nightmare, and his legs refused to obey him.

"*Run . . . ,*" Serge screamed, but his voice sounded like a recording slowed down to half speed.

The creature was close now. Mason could hear something like laughter, could see the shadow falling around him, could even smell an otherworldly odor that reminded him of the smoking stink of a dentist's drill carving into teeth.

It has me, he thought. *There's nothing I can do because it already has me.*

There was a flash of green flame, a sound like tree branches snapping in a thunderstorm, and both boys were suddenly pushed aside and thrown into the grass. Mason tumbled and spun, and when he finally stopped, he was looking up into Mr. Crow's face, still goofy and grinning. The scarecrow had grabbed one of the triplet monster's ghostly-white arms, and he was fighting to hold on to it. The pumpkin's smile never faltered, not even when the grotesque head darted down like a bullet and smashed straight through Mr. Crow's chest, taking a bite out of his tree root ribs. For a moment, the pumpkin head turned toward the boys as if asking for help, and then the triplet monster tossed Mr. Crow's body aside.

"No!" Serge yelled, and he started forward, machete in

hand, before Mason grabbed him by the shirt and pulled him back. Mason's heart ached, but there was nothing to be done.

"We have to run!"

The words had barely left his mouth when the awful creature turned its gaze on them once more. Mason and Serge were defenseless. Their weapons, which had once seemed so dangerous, felt like toothpicks now, and neither boy could move under the insane gaze of that creature from beyond.

Go ahead, Mason thought. *Please, just let it be quick.*

A sudden splash of light fell on them, and Mason was blinded by a pair of headlights from the street. The world was still slow, still hazy, but a horn honked as something black and sleek raced past him, missing him by just a few feet. There was a crash followed by an alien scream inside his head, and the spell he was under suddenly broke. His body returned to his control, and he scrambled up and then leaned over to help Serge back to his feet. His mind ached, but in front of him was an amazing, impossible sight. The giant creature had fallen over on the opposite side of the street and was flailing to get back upright. The tinted window of the truck that had sideswiped it rolled down, and Becca peeked out, grinning. Serge started laughing hysterically.

Mari leaned over Becca's lap. "Get in! Hurry!"

They never looked back. Both boys leapt into the bed of the truck, and Serge slapped the back window.

"Go, go, go!"

The truck slipped into gear, and the tires squealed. A few seconds later, the back window slid open and Mari poked her head out.

"What in the world is that thing?" she shouted.

"No clue," Mason yelled, "but it's chasing us, so I guess we did a good job!"

By then, the triplet monster was back up on its arms. The grotesque head turned and cast its cold yellow gaze in the truck's direction. Becca looked in the rearview mirror.

"Don't look at it!" Serge screamed. "It'll mess you up. Just go!"

Becca floored it, spinning a wild doughnut in the yard, and cut a path toward the center of town. Mason looked back and saw the massive monstrosity giving chase. He was still struggling to make sense of what he was seeing. Its arms and head were totally disconnected from each other, and the bodies of the triplets dangled loosely in the air. The only thing holding the creature together was the triplets' held hands. Horrified, Mason realized that he was only seeing part of a much larger creature.

"Please, drive fast!" he yelled.

"I'm trying!" Becca yelled back.

The truck swerved and clipped a brick mailbox, sending a shower of rocky bits into the back of the truck.

Serge leaned his head into the open window. "Do you know how to drive?"

"A little," Becca said. "My mom lets me drive around parking lots."

She hit another mailbox.

"Empty parking lots," she added. The truck roared, jumped a curb, and turned right into the town square. Mason was still looking backward, watching the beast keep a steady pace with heavy strides of its long arms. It leapt over fences, flipped cars, and wreaked havoc on anything that stood in its way.

"Look at the square!" Mari cried.

For the first time that night, every monster was in the same place. There were hundreds of them, an army of horns, tentacles, teeth, claws, and grotesque faces gathered around the fountain. And in the center, hovering a dozen feet off the ground next to the statue of Bacchus, the Red Witch held court.

"Any ideas?" Becca asked as she turned the truck around the first corner of the square. The monsters were starting to look toward the sound of the truck, and in a few short seconds, they would see the impossible beast chasing them. Mason saw the creature slip and fall into a storefront, completely wiping it out and disappearing into the store itself.

Not much time, Mason thought desperately. *But maybe just enough.*

"Pull over!" he yelled.

"Are you crazy?" Becca asked.

"Just do it!"

She cut the wheel to one side, and the truck came to a stop in front of Benson's. Mason leapt out and ran to the passenger side.

"Drive toward the fountain," he said. "That thing will follow you, and we'll see if these monsters like to play nice with each other. Once they clear out, I'll go for the heart."

Mari flung the door open and leapt out, crowbar in hand.

"I'm going with you," she said.

"But . . . you can't . . ."

"No time to argue," she said. "You need backup, and I'm pretty sure it's safer out here than in that truck." She glanced back at Becca. "No offense."

"None taken," Becca said.

Mari looked at Serge. "You two stick together. Go!"

There was no time for anything but action. No time to think, no time to plan, only time to react. Mason could hear glass and metal breaking as the creature emerged from the storefront. He followed Mari to the front of Benson's to hide as Serge hopped out of the truck bed and into the front seat. The truck roared and sped away, and a few seconds later, the monster followed.

CHAPTER 24

The Hero of This Story

Serpa had led the throng of monsters to the fountain. The night had been bumpy, but when she saw their satisfied, blood-streaked faces, the witch knew it was worth every hiccup.

She held her cane aloft and lifted gently off the ground until she towered above even the largest monsters.

This is where I belong, she mused as she looked down at them. *On top.*

"My friends," she said as they quieted at the sight of her. "To another successful year!"

The monsters roared in approval, and Serpa basked in it, letting the sound of it wash over her. When they fell silent again, she smiled.

"Every year has its share of ups and down. Some maiming, some beheading. But it's all in good fun. I sincerely hope that each of you will return next year. I'm certain it will be the best—"

A shriek ripped through the square and the witch turned to see a truck barreling toward them. She glowered down from her perfect perch on top of the world and a single word escaped her hateful lips.

"Children."

It was a scene out of a movie. The truck raced straight toward the fountain, and the entire horde of monsters turned to look at it.

"Now, *that's* a distraction," Mari said. "Come on."

She and Mason leapt from their hiding place and ran across the road to take cover behind a brick half wall. Mason was transfixed by the chaos unfolding in front of them. The fountain, which rose up like a tower of marble and bronze, was only a hundred yards or so away. It took just a few seconds for the truck to reach the throng of monsters. Mason held his breath.

"I really hope that thing doesn't care who it eats," he said.

The truck headed directly for the center of the horde, but at the last second it veered to one side. The triplet monster didn't even try to swerve. It ran straight into the ocean of snarling mouths and claws. The truck swerved, leapt over the sidewalk, and disappeared around a corner and out of sight.

The monsters were right to be afraid. The creature's giant hands stomped into the center of the crowd and lifted up a fistful of hairy, scaly bodies. The misshapen head stretched and distorted to allow half a dozen monsters into its mouth at once, like a snake swallowing an egg. The unlucky monsters were dead in seconds, and the others fanned out in all directions, terrified that they'd be next. Above them all, the witch hovered and screeched as flames danced from the end of her staff. A ball of blue fire launched forward and exploded against the side of the triplet monster's face, but it didn't even seem to notice as it stomped a path around the fountain, attacking anything that moved. The witch swept along after it, trying to return order to the insanity that had been unleashed on her perfect little world.

"I can't believe it," Mari said as she and Mason dashed toward the fountain. "The coast is actually clear. The plan is *actually* working."

That's right, Mason thought. *We're going to do this. We're going to save Meg and fix this town once and for all.*

He thought back to the clown, to his moment of triumph, to the exhilaration of action. This was like the movies he watched, where the odds were impossible, where a happy ending seemed unreachable, but somehow the hero found a way. Only this was *his* story.

His movie.

And he was the hero.

"Come on," he said, picking up speed, running like he hadn't run since he was eight years old. The field was empty. They dashed across it, and when Mason reached the fountain, he peered down into it. He had gazed into that dark, mossy water hundreds of times in the real Pearl, but it never looked like this. The water glowed softly as if a bottomless blue light was shining from somewhere deep within. He reached down, his fingers an inch from the surface.

"Wait," Mari said, stopping Mason's hand and touching the water with one end of her crowbar. The second it skimmed the surface, it disappeared from sight. She pulled the crowbar back, eyes wide.

"This is it!" she said. "Gloom was right—this is the way out!"

Mason looked up at the statue, which rose some twenty feet above them. The fountain was divided into four pieces by narrow bridges that ran from the rim to the pedestal in the center. Once, when he was a little kid, he'd tried to walk out to the center while his parents were distracted. He had ended up slipping and falling in. He walked all the way home soaked and crying. If he slipped this time, there'd be no second chance.

He took a deep breath, steadying himself. "I'll see if the heart is up there."

"Okay," Mari said. "Hurry!"

Mason ran to one bridge and stepped up. In the distance, he could hear roars of pain and fear mixed with the sounds of metal bending and bricks tumbling to the ground.

He had to stay focused to keep from falling into the blue water. The bridge was only about a foot wide, and it was made of smooth, rounded marble that was slick with water and moss.

I got this, he thought as he placed one foot on the stone and began to walk. *I'm the hero of this story. . . .*

"Mason!" Mari yelled. "Look out!"

Just as he turned to see why she had screamed, something swatted him hard across the back. Mason yelped and fell forward onto the narrow bridge. He gripped it with both hands as he tried to keep from falling into the watery portal below. When he looked back up, he was face to face with the werewolf, the monster that had stalked Mari's mother. Its face was bloody and its eyes were full of rage as it perched on the edge of the fountain. It glared down at Mason and snarled before tilting its head up to howl at the sky. Blood dripped from one of the wolf's eyes and something silvery glinted in the gash above its eye socket.

What's it doing? Mason thought as he glanced over at Mari. The creature had him, and it could easily kill him. The terror on Mari's face told him she knew full well who that howl was summoning.

"She's coming," Mari said.

CHAPTER 25

The Guardian of UnderPearl

The children were behind this. Serpa knew it the second that truck barreled into the square.

How she hated children.

She knew that the only real way to handle the situation was to try to usher the triplets to some dark corner of the town and wait for them to calm down and recede back within themselves. Her last resort, of course, was to end the spell early and leave all the monsters and mayhem stuck inside UnderPearl, but that was a last resort. There was an end game to all of this, the thing she had been working toward for hundreds of years, and a mishandled crisis could ruin it all.

I must keep order, she thought.

She flew behind the triplets, trying her best to minimize the damage to her guests. She whispered a series of spells so quickly that it was impossible to separate one from the other. She tossed a little hairy potato monster into a yard a second before it was flattened. She flung a ball of blue flame that struck the triplet creature in the face just as its jaws were about to close on a black-cloaked vampire. She lifted a fire truck and used it to block a side street, funneling the monster away from the horde of monsters. In between spells, she floated over the crowd and gave her fastest apologies as she tried to keep pace with the triplet monster.

"So sorry . . . you'll have to forgive me. . . . This never happens, really!"

The giant creature barreled out of the square, heading north toward the larger neighborhoods. It would be quieter there, and once the triplets calmed down she might be able to—

That was when Serpa heard the howl. Her wolf had been missing for hours, but she knew he was still loyal, even if no one else was. There was more in a wolf's howl than most humans could hope to comprehend, and when she heard it, there was little doubt.

He had them.

There was something else in that howl, though, a masked pain that told her the wolf had been injured. The rest of the monsters were in disarray, running for their lives. She needed help. The children were a nuisance, nothing she couldn't handle of course, yet they had somehow managed to evade her. Serpa stopped her flight and let the triplet creature stomp away from her. She would handle the triplets after the matter with the children was settled, once and for all.

She held the staff to her mouth and whispered into the

strange little face. The wooden eyebrows shot up. He couldn't speak, but the message was clear.

Are you sure?

"Do it," she said.

The staff obeyed, and the spell rang out, across the remains of the tiny town, toward the protector of UnderPearl. The spiders in Serpa's hair began to crawl from their hiding places, walking up to lock their legs around her head and make a living crown. This was her last and greatest trick, the card she kept up her sleeve in case of just such a moment. She flew back toward the fountain, led by the sound of the howling wolf.

It was time to end this.

Mason was dead. He and Mari both were. He tried to think of a way that they might escape the wolf, but none came to mind. The beast was too wary of the narrow bridge to venture out onto it, but that didn't matter. Even by doing nothing, it had them. The longer they waited, not making a move, the closer the witch would get.

"What do we do?" Mari yelled.

"I'm working on it," Mason said.

"Work faster, please."

Mari held the crowbar in front of her, attempting to draw the werewolf away from Mason. The creature was a good ten feet from her and could still have easily ripped her to shreds, but instead it gripped the edge of the fountain with its claws and stood its ground. With a sinking feeling, Mason realized that he was the target.

Because I'm closer to the heart, he thought.

Mari took a step forward. The wolf turned and growled but refused to retreat.

"I have an idea," Mari said to Mason. "Trust me!" She turned and ran in the opposite direction, circling the fountain to the next bridge, a quarter of the way across from the one Mason was on.

"What are you doing?" he asked.

"You keep him busy!" she yelled as she jumped up onto the bridge, leaping as lightly as a deer.

"Wait!" Mason cried. "I'm supposed to be the hero of the story!"

She reached the base of the fountain and looked back at him. Mason realized that his internal monologue had escaped from his mouth, and he had never felt sillier.

"What the *heck* are you talking about?"

"Nothing!"

The wolf was growling now, and it took a tentative step onto the bridge.

"I said keep it busy. . . . I'm going for the stone!" Mari yelled.

Mason raised up onto his hands and knees and started crawling quickly toward the center of the fountain, the sheathed sword still in one hand. He managed to scramble to his feet, almost dropping the sword as he did so. The werewolf growled again, and he drew the blade from its sheath with a *shing*. He looked away for a moment to check on Mari, who was clambering up the series of pedestals at the base of the statue. When Mason looked back again, the werewolf, as agile as it was silent, was halfway across the bridge.

"Climb faster!" he yelled as he swung the sword, missing the werewolf by a few feet. "Please!"

"I'm trying!"

The werewolf snarled and stalked forward, one silent foot at a time. Now that it was closer, Mason could see just how dangerous it was. Its sinewy muscles were tensed, and he felt like a deer being hunted by a tiger.

"Get back!" he yelled, swinging the sword wildly.

The wolf lowered itself just as the sword whipped through the air over its head. Then, with an impossibly powerful burst of strength, it leapt forward and swatted the sword from Mason's hands. Another paw followed the first, catching Mason in the chest and pinning him against the cold marble. It all happened in less than a second, and when Mason opened his eyes again, the wolf was glaring down at him. The boy who just a few minutes ago had felt like a hero now felt more like a child than ever. The wolf kneeled over him and howled in triumph before it prepared to bite into Mason's throat.

All at once, Mason heard the crackling of dry twigs, and a moment later, a wave of brown vines wrapped around the werewolf's neck. It howled as it was pulled backward toward the bridge, and Mason sat up to see Mr. Crow slumped against the edge of the fountain. He had one arm outstretched, and the vines had slithered along the bridge as silent as a tangle of snakes.

The werewolf bit and snapped and clawed at the thick roots, but there was no getting away as Mr. Crow reeled him in like a fish on a line, pulling him along the bridge, off the fountain, and onto the ground. When Mason finally stood up, he could see it all. The scarecrow was a mangled mess, hanging on just long enough to help his friends one final time. With a last burst of strength, Mr. Crow reached his roots up and dragged the wolf underground, filling its mouth and eyes with dark soil. The creature let out one last howl before vanishing into the earth, never to be seen again.

Mr. Crow gazed up at Mason, the flickering green light within him growing weaker. The pumpkin head drooped and rested on the edge of the fountain, and when Mr. Crow looked back up at Mason, he was still smiling. Mason smiled back, and a moment later, the green light in the triangle eyes blinked out. All that remained was a pile of sticks and a crumbling pumpkin.

"I'm sorry," Mason whispered as his heart broke for the pitiful monster. He turned back to the fountain and looked up at Mari, who was looking down on the scene from halfway up the statue, her eyes shining with tears.

"Go," Mason said, grief choking his voice. It all came down to Mari to save them now. "You can get to the top!"

Mari wiped her eyes and started climbing again, using the statue itself as a ladder. Soon, she was sitting atop Bacchus's broad shoulders. She gingerly leaned forward, peering into the cup that the statue held.

"Can you see anything?" Mason asked.

"There's something in the cup," she said as she flattened

herself out and began to slide forward. "I think . . . maybe I can reach it."

There was a sudden rush of wind, and Mason shielded his eyes for a moment. When he opened them, the Red Witch was hovering next to Mari, her cloak billowing like a bloody cloud, her head crowned with a tangle of spiders.

"That . . . is . . . *enough*."

As she spat out the last word, one bony white hand darted forward and yanked Mari up by a fistful of hair. Mari screamed and instinctively reached up, grabbing hold of the witch's hand while locking her legs around the statue's massive arm to keep from falling. She was trapped like that for a moment, caught between falling and being carried off.

Oh no, Mason thought. *We're done.*

"You know," the witch said as she gazed calmly down at Mason, "I've *always* hated children, even my own. That mewling creature was the first one I tested this little spell on. I didn't know if it would work, but oh . . . the taste of that candy was *amazing*."

"Let her go!" Mason yelled helplessly.

"Please . . . ," Mari begged as she hung on for dear life.

"I've got a plan for both of you," Serpa continued. "I could just leave you here and let you drift around for eternity after I end the spell. But you've been too much trouble. I want this to *hurt*."

Mari was wriggling, trying to get her hair free from the witch's iron grip, and Mason's stomach turned over at the pain etched across her face.

"Speaking of which," Serpa said, "here he comes."

She pointed her cane to the east, and Mason turned and gasped. The garden spider had returned, and it stomped into the square like a toddler walking into a carefully built cityscape of toy building blocks, ready to knock down everything in its path.

"I have bigger plans than just this town," Serpa said, "spells that I've been testing for a hundred years or more. Spells that will turn every child on the face of the planet into candy with a wave of my hand. It will be a glorious day to behold, but unfortunately, you two won't be around to see it."

The witch held up her staff, and the odd little face grinned.

That's what she uses, Mason thought. *She's controlling the spider with it.*

"Come forth, my friend," she said. "It's your turn to have a treat. Start with the boy first. He'll make a fine meal, I'm sure."

The spider lumbered to the edge of the fountain and easily stepped over the pool of water. Its many eyes were the size of dinner plates, and they shined like black mirrors. Its fangs dripped with venom, and its mouth trembled in anticipation of the meal to come.

"Mari!" Mason yelled as he pressed back against the statue. "The staff!" He pointed toward the witch and Mari looked at her.

You got one chance, he thought. *We got one chance.*

Serpa scowled. "That's enough from the two of you—"

Before the witch could finish, Mari went for it. She leaned over and grasped the staff with both hands, at the same moment uncurling her legs from around the statue. Her sudden weight yanked the cane from the witch's hands, and for a moment Mari dangled, held aloft by a handful of her own hair. She screamed as the witch's grip failed her, sending Mari dropping a full ten feet to the base of the statue.

Mason was next to her a second later. The spider filled the sky above them, and Mari barely had enough breath to croak as she handed him the cane.

"This better work. . . ."

Mason raised the cane and smashed it against the marble pedestal. It splintered and snapped in two. An inhuman scream filled the air, and for a split second, an awful little face hovered before Mason like a wisp of smoke. It looked surprisingly happy, its tiny eyes shining, before it dissipated and vanished. The spirit that had been doing the witch's bidding for untold years was finally free from her grasp.

"*Nooo!*" Serpa screamed. "Do you know what you've done?"

She dropped down on a gust of wind right between Mason and the spider, and wrapped her cold, bony fingers around Mason's neck. He pushed her back, but any hope that she would become frail without her staff was immediately dashed. She was still stronger than Mason, and she smashed his head against the pedestal.

"You think you can stop me?" she spat as she clawed at his neck. "This town belongs to me, and these children are mine to feast on!"

"*One . . . little . . . thing . . . ,*" Mason choked out.

"What are you babbling about?" she asked, pulling him closer.

"Spider venom," he whispered, "liquefies the insides of insects."

"What?" the witch said.

He nodded jerkily to the gigantic spider behind her. The crown of spiders on her head broke as they dropped to the statue, fleeing for cover. Mason knew then that his hunch had been right. The spiders were no longer the witch's to command. The giant spider that defended her town was still hungry, and it would settle for whoever was closest. Eight cold, glassy eyes leaned down so close that Mason could see his reflection in them, and a pair of fangs the size of machetes sunk into the witch's back. Her eyes grew wide, and bloody tears raced down both cheeks as she gazed at Mason, the boy who had been her undoing.

"There will be consequences," she groaned softly. *"Now . . . suffer, little children . . ."*

The Red Witch of Pearl was lifted from the fountain, soon to be wrapped in silk and eaten. The satisfied spider dragged its prey away, eager to return to the safety of its web, the delectable morsel intact.

CHAPTER 26

Mason's Choice

The square was silent except for the sound of Mason and Mari fighting to catch their breath. The spider was gone, and with it, the Red Witch of Pearl. Somehow, they had actually pulled it off.

"You okay?" Mason asked, offering Mari his hand. She had taken quite a fall, and she winced as he helped her to her feet.

"Never better, hero."

Mason could feel himself turn red, but she smiled and shook her head.

"I'm not messing with you," she said, giving him a pat on the shoulder. "You actually did good."

"Well . . . I couldn't have done it without—"

There was a burst of laughter behind him, and Mason spun around to see a filthy baseball player and a zombie

230

cheerleader with most of her makeup worn off limping toward the fountain. They were holding hands.

"I guess that's one way to deal with a witch," Serge said, before doubling over and almost falling down.

"We almost died," Becca said, laughing hysterically. "Like ten times or something."

"I wish you could have seen it, Mason," Serge said. "It was mayhem. Crushed buildings. Monsters running and scream-ing. You would have loved it."

"I flipped a truck!" Becca said excitedly.

"She flipped a truck!" Serge added.

Their laughter was infectious, and soon Mason joined in. Mari scooted herself up to lean against the pedestal, and she laughed as well, though not nearly as loudly.

"Oh, that hurts," she said, clutching her side.

"We need to get you to a doctor," Mason said.

"Him too," Becca said, gesturing to Serge.

"I think my ankle's broken," Serge said.

"What happened to the triplets?" Mason asked after a few moments.

"We lost them in the crowd before we flipped the truck," Becca said.

"Hopefully that's the last of them," Mason replied.

"Oh . . . ," Serge said suddenly as he noticed the pumpkin resting against the fountain. "Mr. Crow . . ." He walked over to the remains of the scarecrow.

"He didn't make it," Mason said. "But he saved us."

"He saved all of us," Serge replied.

Mason would never have called his best friend the sensitive type, but it seemed like the glass shell around Serge's heart was broken at the sight of the scarecrow's remains. He held his hand to his face and silently began to weep. Becca leaned on his shoulder and patted his back. "I'll let you do the climbing this time," Mari told Mason as she wiped her own eyes.

He climbed quickly but carefully, making sure he had a good foothold each step of the way. Soon, Mason was at the statue's summit, and after a few moments of stretching out across the arm of Bacchus, the god of wine and celebrations, he reached into the cup. Inside, he felt something small and irregularly shaped. He wrapped his fingers tightly around it, almost dizzy with relief. He didn't open his iron grip until he was back on steady ground, and when he did, the sight of what he held made him gasp. He'd never seen anything like it. The gem was made of a series of overlaid geometric patterns, like a tiny maze in his palm. The entire stone glowed with a literal rainbow of colors.

"Wow."

"Wow," Mari echoed, leaning over his hand.

"A rainbow bismuth," Becca said. "You actually can grow them. I never did it myself. It's pretty complicated. Someone put some real effort into that thing."

"This is it," Mason said. "I crush this, and this entire place disappears for good."

"Let's get out of here before we do that," Mari said.

"Wait," Mason said, his stomach plummeting. "The candy! Serge, do you still have it?"

"I got you, remember?" Serge said, reaching into his

pocket. He opened his hand and showed Mason the delicately wrapped piece of candy. Tears welled in Mason's eyes when he looked at it. He held out his hand and Serge dropped it into his palm.

That's her, Mason thought. *That's what's left of my sister.*

"You did it," Mason said.

"We did it," Serge said. "All of us."

"Thank you," Mason added. "Thank . . . all of you."

He looked from face to face. They were tired. They were bloody. They were all in need of a good shower. But somehow, they had done it.

"So," Mason said, clearing his throat, "any idea how this . . . candy works?"

"I can handle that part."

They turned around. Gloom sat on the edge of the pedestal.

"You're sneaky, you know that?" Mason asked.

"Oh, I'm *well* aware," she said. "Give the candy to me."

Mason limped over, his heart in his throat. There was no way of knowing what might happen next.

"We've done everything right," he said, uncertainty rising in him as he held out his hand. "It would be a shame for this story to still be a tragedy when all's said and done."

"The Red Witch of Pearl is gone," Gloom said. "You took care of my problem. Now I'll take care of yours."

She plucked the candy out of his palm and opened the bag at her side. Mason glimpsed the inside for only a brief moment, but in that moment, he saw an infinite plain, a sky filled with twinkling stars, a sea of white-capped waves, and a forest of endlessly tall trees. His heart ached to see more, but Gloom closed the bag a second later.

"Your sister will be waiting for you," she said. "Right on your front porch."

"And my mother?" Mari asked.

Gloom smiled, but for once, there was no mischief in it.

"Like Mason said, you did everything right. You'll have to just go through that portal and see for yourself."

"I'll go first," Becca said. "Just to make sure this works. I wouldn't want Serge to break his other ankle."

Light was beginning to appear in the sky, but it was a strange light, a sunrise inside of a dead tree. Becca perched on the edge of the fountain and dipped her toe into it.

"My shoe's not wet." She took a deep breath. "Well, here goes nothing."

She hopped gently off the edge and, without so much as a single splash, vanished.

"Your turn," Mason said, helping Mari to her feet.

"Easy," she said, wincing. He held her hand as she stepped down from the pedestal and into the water. "I can't touch the bottom," she said.

"I think that's normal," he said. "As normal as anything is at this point."

She let go of his hand and silently slipped down into the fountain.

"Your turn, big man," Mason said. It took Serge a moment to get his sore foot up, but once he did, he looked up and smiled.

"So," Serge said, "Saitama versus Superman. Who you got?"

Mason grinned and shook his head.

"I'll have to get back to you on that," he said. "We really did it, didn't we?"

Serge smiled. "You owe me big." Then he slipped into the water, grinning the whole time, leaving Mason alone in this strange world, with this strange girl.

"You know, I can see right through you mortals," Gloom said. "You're like little glass jars, but you're all filled up with something different. Your jar is filled to the top with this sense of heroism. You thought you were the star of this story, but the truth is, without all four of you, none of you would have made it out."

Mason knew she was right—it was the group that made the difference. Heroes, real heroes, couldn't do it alone.

"You know, I started this night out with really only one friend," Mason said with a smile. "I'd say that was a pretty good night, all things considered."

He held out the stone. "When I crush this, it's over, right?"

"Yes," Gloom said, "but the witch wasn't lying. There *will* be consequences."

Mason swallowed hard and tried to work up the courage to ask the question that had floated up in his mind.

"My friend," he said gently. "Marco . . . is he . . . ?"

"I told you earlier that there was no coming back."

Mason nodded.

"But . . . he's safe now. He's no longer stuck in between. I can't say any more, but just know that he's okay. Everything is okay."

Mason sniffed and asked, "Will you . . . tell him I said hi?"

"Sure."

The sun began to crest over Gloom's shoulders.

"My time is almost up," she said. "And you, Mason Miller, have got one more choice to make." The sun began to shine through her, and her face went all shimmery and hazy.

"What choice?"

She nodded over his shoulder, and Mason turned to see for himself. The monsters had returned. They were gathered around the fountain like a congregation, their eyes all locked on him. Mason looked at Gloom, who opened her palm and pointed at it, reminding Mason of exactly what he was holding. He gazed down at the strange rock in his hand.

"It's your move," she said, "and before you ask, I don't *know* the right answer. Maybe there isn't one. Making life isn't easy, but making death is just as tough. I'll leave it up to you to decide."

With that, she was gone, faded out of existence, but her voice lingered.

"Make your choice," she whispered, "and whatever you do, make peace with it."

Only Mason remained, a lone human surrounded by what looked like every monster in the world. He scrambled down and grabbed Mari's crowbar, then placed the shining stone on the pedestal.

"Nobody move!" he yelled. "If I crush this, you'll all disappear! Forever. Do you understand?"

The plan was right there in front of him, so simple, so *easy*. All he had to do was jump through the exit and immediately smash the stone on the other side. With a simple swing of the crowbar, these inhuman *things* would be gone for good.

That's what they deserve, he thought. *And that's what a hero would do . . . right?*

The faces looking at him were grim. The creatures could have killed him in a thousand different ways, each bloodier and viler than the last. This was every villain he'd ever watched on the big screen, every obscure monster from his dreams.

The mummies and vampires. The giant eyeball on a stalk. The bird-headed man with the pet monkey. Furry and slimy things. Beasts with no eyes and slithering things with dozens of eyes. The clown who stood with his own grinning head tucked under his arm. The triplets, who had calmed themselves down, and stood hand in hand, mouths restitched.

They all looked to him and waited for his choice.

Mr. Crow still lay with the remnants of his head resting against the fountain. There was no magic that would bring him back, but a simple truth remained. If the witch hadn't brought Mr. Crow to life, Mason would be dead.

Life and death, Mason thought. *Just do it. Just end this once and for all.*

His eyes were watering.

They're just monsters.

Yes, they were monsters. Yes, they could, and probably would, kill him if they got the chance. But he couldn't hate them, any more than he could hate a shark for attacking a surfer or a spider for biting the foot that steps on it. There was good in Mr. Crow, and maybe there could be good in them too. The monster he saved today could be the monster that saved him tomorrow.

He looked down at the stone and held his breath.

"I'm going through," Mason told them. "And I'll let you all leave too. But then this place is gone. Forever. So, you can't come back. This town is off-limits. Do you understand?"

They stared at him, silent. A woman near the front of the pack stepped forward. Her face was a mesh of scales and her hair was a writhing bundle of snakes.

"Do we have your word, human?"

Her voice was full of reverence, as if she was making some secret, magical pledge that could never be broken.

"Yes."

The snake-haired woman nodded, and Mason jumped into the fountain.

The world turned upside down once more, and he felt himself falling, rising, and then finally standing on solid ground. He was back in Pearl, the *real* Pearl, and he stood in the center of the fountain, in water up to his knees. The others stood just outside the fountain, and as Mason appeared, Serge reached over the half wall and wrapped him in a fierce hug.

"What took you so long?"

The sun was up now, but the town was utterly silent. A few people remained in the park, but they all looked dead, more or less. Beer cans littered the ground, and it was clear that the hardest partyers had slept wherever they dropped.

"What in the world?" Mason asked.

"I know," Mari said. "It's like the entire town is paused or something."

"No," Mason said. "It's more than that. It's her spell. She had to make sure that all the monsters could leave, so she had to put everyone in town to sleep."

"Why did you take you so long?" Becca asked. But Mason wasn't paying attention to her.

"Oh no, move," he said as he leapt out of the fountain.

"What is it?" Serge asked.

"Just scoot back," Mason said as he dragged the group away from the edge.

They stared at the water long enough for the surface to go smooth and still. Then the first rotting hand emerged and slapped the side of fountain. The zombies pulled their way out first, emerging into the bright sun, their eyes half-closed.

"Mason, what did you do?" Mari whispered.

"Just back up," Mason said. "Give them space."

A dozen zombies clawed their way out, and though each of them stared at the four kids, none of them made a move to attack. Instead, they slowly marched in a line toward the woods. The last zombie, a man in a gray suit with a red tie, wore Serge's baseball cap. The other monsters soon followed the zombie, creating a procession of monstrosities large and small. Mason watched them all, clutching the gem as they passed.

"Why did you do that?" Becca whispered. "Why did you let them escape?"

The woman with snakes for hair slithered out and glared at them, followed by the rat man and the little hairy potato creature. A squat creature with no skin and tiny, beady eyes tumbled over the side and glanced up at the group of four with a polite little bow. The monster almost seemed to be thanking them. One after another, they all emerged and slunk away, back to the woods, back to their dens and lairs, to await the night once more. The last ones to appear were the triplets. The awful thing inside them was pacified for now, and their mouths remained firmly stitched.

"What the heck?" Serge said, hiding behind Mason when he saw them.

The trio climbed out of the fountain and bowed in perfect unison before pattering off and out of sight.

"Why would you let something like that go?" Serge asked.

"I thought about Mr. Crow," Mason replied as he walked over to the fountain and placed the rock down on a flat spot. "Maybe there's something good in some of them. Maybe not. Either way, it's not my place to decide whether they should live or die."

Serge reached into his pocket and pulled something out.

"Speaking of which." He held a handful of white pumpkin seeds. "I got them from Mr. Crow when you were climbing the statue," he said, eyes shining. "Maybe if I plant them . . . something will grow."

Mason nodded, touched by Serge's hope.

"What if they come back?" Mari asked, gazing warily at the retreating monsters.

"They won't," Mason said, remembering the snake woman's somber words as he carefully held the crowbar over the stone. When he brought the crowbar down, the rock split into a dozen pieces. The air suddenly felt heavy and thick, and the world grew silent. Then, like a breeze, the feeling passed, and the morning sun shined all the brighter.

A man in his early twenties who was passed out less than thirty feet away sat up and began to rub his temples.

"Look," Serge said. All around them, the world was unpausing.

"The spell is broken," Mason said.

The witch's words echoed through his mind. *There will be consequences.*

"Let's go home," he said as a pit formed in his stomach. Gloom had made it clear that Meg would be waiting, but he needed to see her with his own two eyes.

They walked away from the square as quickly as they could manage, limping and holding each other up as they went. Serge had to lean on Mason's shoulder to stay on his feet. All around them, the town was beginning to return, but it felt different somehow. Pearl wasn't just waking up from a hard night of partying, it was waking up from a much longer and darker sleep, a nightmare it hadn't even known was happening.

"Becca," Mari said as they walked, "go home. Your house is so far out of the way."

Becca looped her arm under Mari's and leaned on her shoulder.

"My mom can get me later," Becca said. "I want to stay with you until . . . until you get home."

Mason understood. Until Mari saw her mom again, there would be no sense of peace.

The group walked onto Orville Avenue to find the usual disaster area. The street was orange with pumpkin guts, some of which had been crushed to pulp under the tires of passing cars. Trash speckled every yard, even the neatest and most well-kept ones. As they walked, doors began to slowly open as people faced the morning with bleary eyes. Mr. Kirby, as grim as ever, already stood in his yard, scooping up trash. He glared at them as they passed, as if these four beaten, shabby-looking kids had personally thrown the trash into his yard.

"Don't make eye contact," Serge said as the four of them shuffled quickly past.

About a block from Mari's, they passed a small house on a corner. The door was flung open and a frantic mother raced out, screaming.

"Abbie! *Abbie!* Has anyone seen my daughter?"

People were gathering now, emerging from their homes to witness the commotion.

"Oh no," Mason whispered.

"What is it?" Serge asked.

"That's Abbie Purdom's mom. Abbie was the little girl who disappeared last year."

There will be consequences. The mother was hysterical, but her scream was drowned out by another voice, this one belonging to an older gentleman a few houses down.

"Jake?" he screamed. "Has anyone seen my son?"

Soon, the street was alive with a truly terrible sound, the unbridled fear of parents who'd lost the most precious thing in the world.

"I don't understand," Becca said.

"The spell has been on this town for a long time," Mason said, horrified. "They're finally waking up and realizing their kids are gone."

He held a hand to his mouth, suddenly feeling as if he might be sick. "I didn't want this."

"You didn't do it," Serge reminded him.

His friend was right, but in that moment, it didn't seem to matter. What the witch had done to this town was unbearably cruel, but she wasn't here to see the aftermath. Without saying a word, the four of them picked up their pace, hoping that they could outrun the sound of sadness that chased them up the street. A few minutes later, they came to the familiar brick building at the corner. The door still stood ajar.

"We should all go in," Serge said.

"No," Mari insisted, wiping her eyes. "It's fine. Really."

She stood and stared at the door for a long while as Becca gently patted her shoulder.

"I can go in first if you want me to," Becca said.

Mari shook her head, then took a step forward before pausing.

"I can't do it . . . ," she said.

Just then, the door flew open and an exhausted, wild-eyed woman stepped out.

"Mari!" she yelled as she ran forward and engulfed her daughter in a hug that nearly knocked her down. "I was worried sick!"

"Mom," Mari cried, "I'm so glad you're okay!"

"You won't believe the night I had," her mother said, leaning back to inspect her daughter.

"Mine was pretty wild too."

Mari's mother suddenly seemed to notice the others standing there, and she smiled at them. Her hair was still a mess, and her vampire makeup was half gone.

"Becca, what happened?" she said. "You look . . . like a wreck. And are these some new friends?"

Mason and Serge were quickly introduced, and in the frantic few moments that followed, mother and daughter spilled out their insane, impossible nights to each other, culminating with the wolf attack in the bathroom.

"I don't understand how you got away," Mari said. "Mason and I saw the whole thing, and the wolf was already on top of you."

"Silver!" her mother cried. "That message you wrote."

She showed Mari her earring, then showed her other ear, which was bare.

"Your dad got me these, remember? I only wear them on special occasions. Real silver."

Mason remembered the wolf's bloody eye and the metallic glint that shined out from within.

Earring in the eyeball, Mason thought. *That must have stung.*

244

"I just pulled it off and jabbed it into that thing's eye. It took off like a bullet after that."

Mari laughed. Her mother laughed. And the others laughed as well. Mari glanced over at Mason and smiled.

"Silver for werewolves, right?" she asked.

"You got it."

For the first time since that night, Mason felt normal again, but the feeling was overwhelmed by a wave of grief and guilt.

"Ma'am," he said suddenly, "it's really nice to meet you, and I'm glad everything worked out, but . . . I gotta go find Meg."

"Who's Meg?" Mari's mother asked.

"Mom," Mari said, "we'll be back in a minute. I'll explain everything then, but . . . we have to go!"

Her mother protested, but Mason didn't hang around to hear any more. He took off as fast as his exhausted legs could carry him. His house was only a few blocks away, but a stitch grew in his side almost immediately. He glanced back just once, expecting to see nothing but an empty street. Instead, his three friends were right behind him.

The front porch, he thought. *Please let her be there.*

Meg was sitting in one of the rocking chairs, still in her princess costume. From a distance, it looked as if she was sleeping, like she was just another leftover from the wild Halloween night. Mason stopped in his tracks, gasping, barely able to believe the sight. He walked up the stairs slowly before looking back at the others. They were all out of breath, but none of them would be able to rest until they saw with their own eyes.

"What if she doesn't wake up?" Mason asked the group.

For once, none of them had anything to say, and Mason knew that his friends were just as terrified as he was. He knelt down and gently patted his sister on the shoulder. For a moment, she didn't move.

There will be consequences.

Then her eyelids fluttered, blinked, and opened.

"Mason?"

"Yeah, Meg," he said, struggling not to cry. "I'm right here."

"I . . . I think I had a bad dream," she whispered.

"It's okay," he said as tears spilled from his eyes. He picked Meg up and cradled her in his arms, hugging her tighter than he ever had before.

"Probably just too much candy," he said.

CHAPTER 27

Maybe Next Halloween

Mason didn't tell his friends what he was planning. He knew it was foolish to go back into those woods, and even more foolish to go alone, but he was sure that if they knew, they'd try to stop him. A month had passed since Halloween night, and the week that followed was one the people of Pearl would never forget. The police force, already comically small and unprepared for something as huge as the scandal that had rapidly bloomed under their noses, had no answers for the countless reporters who set up shop in town. The questions were huge and mysterious, and the answers remained elusive and unsatisfying. There were already dozens of conspiracy theories online about what had really happened because the official explanations made no sense.

In total, twenty-three residents of Pearl were officially reported as missing in one day, though no one could say why so many parents suddenly decided to report their children missing, especially considering that some of those kids would be nearly forty years old now.

It was nationwide news, at least for a few days. Journalists used phrases like *mass hysteria* to describe what was happening, and there were cameras set up on every street corner giving their reports. School was even canceled for a few days to let things calm down.

Mason wanted to check out the dead tree in the woods sooner, but he didn't dare, not with all the attention. Thankfully, the news moves quickly, and by the end of November, the town was relatively quiet once more. The echoes of what had happened that Halloween night would continue for years, maybe even decades, but life had no choice but to keep moving forward.

His parents were in the living room watching TV when Mason slipped his jacket on and walked quietly down the stairs. He wasn't intending to break any rules, but he still felt a bit like a criminal returning to the scene of a crime. He hadn't done anything wrong, but a heavy feeling of guilt continued to cling to his heart.

"That you, Mason?" his dad asked.

He sighed and poked his head into the living room. "Yep?"

"You going out?"

"I think so," he said. "Not too many days left with the sun still shining."

"You meeting Serge?" his mom asked.

"Yeah. Probably."

"You two stay close to each other," she said, turning back to the TV. "World's gone crazy."

Mason glanced over at Meg, who was curled up on the couch with a book. The feeling of guilt squeezed a bit tighter as it always did whenever he looked at her. He couldn't stop wondering if maybe, somehow, she remembered what had happened. Mason never knew exactly what his sister had gone through that awful night, but it felt like a great kindness that the memory seemed to have left her. He could only hope that the memory was gone for good.

As he walked out into the crisp autumn air, he thought about everything that had happened. Maybe part of the reason he was so nervous about going back was because it would make that whole terrible night real again. It was so easy to put it behind him, to pretend that it *hadn't* happened. Walking back into those woods, to the place where it all began, would put him back there, feeling lost and alone, feeling guilty because he hadn't watched out for Meg like he should have.

Just walk, he thought as he stepped off the porch. *One step at a time.*

The town was back to normal, more or less, but patchy spots of orange still stained the streets. The decorations were long gone, though, which was a big change for Orville Avenue. Usually at least a few people would leave theirs up until nearly Christmas. Not this year. As soon as the reporters had arrived, all the festive fun of Halloween was drained from the place, and the decorations looked more like pieces of evidence, incriminating a town that was deeply ashamed of itself.

Mason passed by Serge's house, refusing to look at it. If he saw his friend gazing back at him out the window, he would lose his nerve and the trip would be over. He needed to do this, and if he didn't do it now, he might never be able to.

When he reached the cul-de-sac where they had first tangled with Mr. Crow, he stopped and looked back for a long time, making sure he wasn't being followed. Then he pressed on, into the woods, and began to trace his way back. He came to the highway and waited to make sure no cars were coming before he dashed across. A few minutes later, he reached the little clearing and saw her.

Mari was sitting on a rock, facing the hollowed-out tree. She had her back to Mason, but she scrambled to her feet as he approached.

"What are you doing here?" he asked, surprised.

"I could ask you the same thing." She sighed deeply, and for a moment he saw what she would look like as an adult, thin and pretty, in a harried sort of way.

"I just needed to come here," Mason said. "To see it for myself."

"Me too," she replied. "I've come here a few times now."

"My mom thinks I'm over at Serge's."

"Why aren't you?"

He shrugged. "He's always with Becca now." He thought about how that must sound and then caught himself. There was a time, not so long ago in fact, that he would have been quite jealous. He smiled and added, "It's cool, though. She makes him happy. That's good enough for me."

"So why did you come here?" Mari asked.

Mason realized he didn't have a good answer.

"To keep an eye on things, I guess. I feel like I'm watching a coin flip, you know? Like I still don't know if it's heads or tails, but instead of falling, it just sort of floats in midair."

He looked up at Mari and laughed. "I'm sure that sounds stupid."

"No, it doesn't," she said. "A doctor told me once that that feeling is called anxiety. It's the kind of thing I thought I understood, like it was freaking out about a test or something. But I really didn't, at least not until my dad died. I do now, though."

Mason sighed. "I keep feeling like I'm going to wake up one morning and find my mom screaming, just like all those parents did when we walked down Orville. I try to play video games or hang out with Serge or whatever, but nothing feels the same. Nothing feels . . . right. That feeling is still there, just kinda . . . waiting."

"I'd hear my mom crying at night for weeks," Mari said. "I don't think she knew I heard her, but I never knew for sure. That was when it felt the worst, just knowing there was this thing I couldn't fix."

"How do you make it go away?" Mason asked.

"I'm not sure you can. I don't think the feeling ever really goes away, but I do think you get a little stronger every day. It's like when you get sick and your immune system gets a little tougher."

Mason nodded, but he didn't feel relieved in any way.

"All right then," he said. "Why did you come out here?"

Mari laughed uncomfortably.

"You promise not to laugh?"

He nodded.

"Well, the first time I came out here, I was like you," she said. "I just needed to see it. I thought it was all out of my system after that, but then . . . well, I got something stuck in my head. Some little, silly thing that I couldn't get out."

"What?"

"The spider," Mari said. "It sounds crazy, but I just got this idea in my head, lying in bed one night about a week ago, thinking about what might have happened to it. I had to come here. To see it for myself."

The woods were quiet for a moment, then Mason let out a laugh of disbelief.

"Let me get this straight," he said. "You came all the way out here because you were concerned *for the spider*."

Mari blushed. "I told you not to laugh."

"Well," he said, "you came all this way. We'd better take a look."

They went back and forth a few times, but Mason eventually agreed to be the one to look in the hollowed-out tree. He poked a stick in first, half expecting it to be snatched out of his hand. When nothing happened, he finally leaned forward to take a peek. It was still filled with spiderwebs, but he didn't see the big garden spider anywhere.

"Well, good news, I'm not getting sucked in," Mason said. "Bad news, I don't see your little buddy—"

"Dude, what are you doing?"

Mason whipped around. To his amazement, Serge and Becca stood at the edge of the grove. Serge was still wearing a plastic boot on his right foot, and he limped carefully forward.

"What are *you* doing here?" Mason asked.

Becca was holding a tiny gardening spade, which she quickly hid behind her back. Serge was holding a bottle of water, and he did the same.

"I think we all have some explaining to do," Mari said.

"Just show them," Becca said. Serge stared down at the ground, and she elbowed him in the side. "Come on, Serge."

He reached into his pocket and pulled out a handful of pumpkin seeds.

"Oh . . . I forgot about those," Mari said.

"Yeah, man, why didn't you tell me?" Mason asked, confused.

"He's being weird about it," Becca said with a grin. She held up the gardening spade. "I told him I'd help him plant them, but he's all embarrassed."

"I just don't know what's going to happen," Serge said. "I . . . didn't want to get everyone's hopes up."

"I can't believe you still have them," Mari said. "I thought maybe they vanished after the spell was broken."

"Me too," Serge said. "I mean, that pumpkin was part of UnderPearl, and that place is long gone. I don't understand it. Maybe when we put it on Mr. Crow, it became part of him."

"Why all the way out here?" Mason asked.

"That was *my* idea," Becca said. "I mean, think about it. We're trying to grow a magic pumpkin guy. This is probably the most magic place we know about."

"The witch is gone," Mason said. "I think the magic is too."

"Look, if you don't want to help, you don't have to," Serge said.

"No . . . I want to help," Mason said.

"Me too," Mari said.

"Okay then," Becca said. "Let's find a spot."

It didn't take long to find a nice, smooth patch of earth a few feet from the tree. They took turns digging it up, and Serge dropped the seeds in himself. When the dirt was packed back in, he drizzled the bottle of water, soaking the spot. When it was all said and done, Mason saw Serge wipe the corner of one eye.

"This is probably stupid," he said. "I don't think anything will grow this late in the year. But even if it doesn't, at least part of Mr. Crow got a decent burial."

"I think that's about all we can ask for," Mason said.

Mari turned away and walked over to the tree once more.

"I'm not going anywhere near that thing," Becca said.

"I just want to double-check something," she said.

"I already looked," Mason said. "I'm telling you, that thing's not—"

"Found it!"

Mason leaned over her shoulder, but she held a hand up. "Give me the shovel." Becca handed it over, and Mari reached down and scooped something up. Then she stepped carefully back and held the shovel up. The others leaned in and stared at it.

"It was hiding," Mari said.

"Whoa . . ."

"I've never seen anything like that."

"Are you sure it's the same one?"

The garden spider was good sized, but not nearly as threatening as when it had towered over them. It had turned bone white. The spots, which had been bright yellow, were now a brilliant red and the eight tiny eyes had turned the color of blood. It looked like the spider had been dipped in paint.

"Whoa," Mason said, half terrified and half fascinated. "It *looks* like her."

They stood in silence, none of them able to deny it.

"What does it mean?" Mari asked.

"I . . . I don't know," Serge replied.

"What if it *is* her?" Becca said. "What if all that magic and misery is in this spider now?"

The spider scuttled slowly and awkwardly to the edge of the shovel, and Mari had to turn it to keep the spider from falling to the ground.

Mari sighed. "Honestly, it just seems like a spider."

A cold breeze blew through the grove, and Mason shivered.

"Aren't garden spiders usually dead by now?" he asked. "We've already had some hard frost. Shouldn't it be gone?" He leaned even closer and took a careful look at the spider. The bloody red eyes stared back at him, but they held no malice. "It's just a spider," he said, and to his surprise, he believed it. "Maybe her magic will keep it alive longer. Maybe it'll turn into something else. Maybe it will even get dangerous at some point, but we'll handle that if the time comes."

He looked at Mari, who was smiling at him. She already knew what he was going to say.

"Your choice," he said.

"Let's put it back," Mari said. "Just let it be."

"We can all come back and check on it," Becca said. "Not every day or anything, but . . . every once in a while."

Serge smiled and pointed down at the patch of dirt.

"We can keep an eye on Mr. Crow too."

The weight that had been on Mason's shoulders wasn't gone, not completely, but when they walked back to town, he felt lighter than he had in weeks. The four of them walked side by side, and when they hit the cul-de-sac, they stopped and took a long look at Orville Avenue.

"Pearl's never going to be the same," Mason said.

"Yeah," Serge answered. "Who knows what next Halloween will be like."

"Maybe next year will be better," Mari said.

"I think so," Mason said, savoring the new lightness in him. "Yeah. It will be."

Serge and Becca said goodbye when they reached his house, and Mason and Mari kept walking together a bit longer. They reached the witch's empty house. Without the decorations, it didn't look scary at all. There was no For Sale sign. No police tape. Mason half expected to see her walk out onto the porch, not as a witch, but as a friendly old woman who blended perfectly into the town. The two of them passed by without a word, and soon enough, they arrived at the corner where Mari lived.

"I guess I'll see you at school. . . ."

"Wait," Mason said. "I want to say something. Something I should have said earlier. Back in UnderPearl, when I said that thing about me being the hero . . ."

Mari turned a little red, and Mason had the feeling that she was actually embarrassed for him.

"Yeah, I remember."

"My whole life was just watching heroes in movies overcome these big obstacles to kill the bad guy and save the day. I had this idea in my mind that I was the hero of this whole thing, but . . . it was you. And Becca. And Serge too. I wouldn't have made it without *all* of you, and Meg wouldn't have either. You all are the reason my sister and I are alive."

Mari thought for a moment, and it seemed to Mason that she was trying to decide whether she wanted to say something. Finally, she spoke.

"My mom would be dead if it wasn't for you," she said. "So . . . you *are* the hero. To me."

Mason grinned, and Mari rolled her eyes.

"Don't let it go to your head!" she said, slapping him on the shoulder.

"I promise," he replied. "See you at school, Mari."

"See you there, Mason Miller."

When Mason walked into the kitchen, his mom and dad were arguing about whether or not his dad could eat expired ketchup.

"Mason, settle this for us," his dad said. "It's a month out of date. Still good, right?"

"He's going to catch the funk if he eats it," his mom replied. Mason looked from one to the other, trying not to laugh.

"I'll leave that up to you two."

Mason dropped his winter coat off in his room and opened the top drawer of his desk. The notebook that had belonged to him and Marco was still there, still frayed and curling. He sat down on the edge of his bed and opened it.

"'The Monster That Ate the World,'" he read aloud. "'By Mason Miller and Marco Diaz.'"

His long-lost friend's name was as clear as it had been the day he wrote it. He skimmed forward a few pages and saw his own words over and over.

Marco Diaz was real. He sat on the edge of the bed for a moment, looking around at all the monsters, all the posters, all of the wonderful horror that had meant so much to him over the years. It had all started with a couple of second graders sneaking a movie they were too young to watch. Mason couldn't help but smile.

"Thanks, Marco."

When he came back into the living room, Meg was still sitting on the couch, but she had given up on the book. Instead, she was watching cartoon reruns with a box of cereal in her lap. On the screen, a young woman with a sword was fighting a skeleton-faced man riding a dragon. Mason sat down next to his sister.

"So, who's winning?" he asked, reaching into the box for a handful of cereal.

"On the show?"

"Yeah," Mason said, smashing the entire handful into his mouth.

"The good guys," Meg said. "They always win."

Mason smiled.

"Yeah . . . I guess they do."

Mason had things he wanted to do, horror movies to watch, video games to play. They could all wait. Instead, he just sat there for a while, listening to his parents go back and forth while Meg dozed on his shoulder. The November wind blew hard against the windows. Winter was on the way, but for now, it was warm and safe inside.

Sometime later, when the sun was gone and night had come once again to Pearl, Mason slipped into a dreamless sleep. And out in the woods, far from human eyes, an oddly colored garden spider crept out from its hiding place and gazed toward the sleeping town.

Acknowledgments

I've been tinkering around with this whole writing thing for over twenty years now, and while I didn't plan on writing books for kids, I'm thrilled that the path veered in this direction. Bringing this book to life was a massive effort, and I want to take a moment to acknowledge the people who helped make it a reality.

First, I want to thank my family, especially my wife, Alicia, who's been forced to read half-finished books for the past few decades. I'm sure at least a few of those rough drafts were painful, but even when I found it hard to believe in myself, she was always there to encourage me and keep me on the right path. I can't thank her enough for that.

Lucky for her I've now moved on to annoying my kids with my endless, rambling ideas. Whether they know it or not, they're part of the family business now, and they have done more to spark my creativity and drive than they will ever know.

None of this would ever have happened if it weren't for my parents' support of my creativity over the years. Their love and encouragement are visible in everything I've ever written. This book in particular is bittersweet because we had to say goodbye to my father while it was being written. He was an uncommonly kind man, and his endless creativity and love of storytelling is alive in every word I write.

I also want to genuinely thank the hard work of everyone on the Delacorte team, especially Wendy and Alison, whose contributions to the book helped to shape it into what you just read. This team was a joy to work with, and they improved the book in profound ways.

I wouldn't have made it here without the hard work and dedication of my agent, Aimee, and the team at Brower Literary. We writers are a strange group, and we need people in our corner to see the potential in that strangeness and to help the rest of the world see it as well. I'm very grateful that Aimee has been that person for me.

And of course, I want to acknowledge all the young readers out there. There are a million different things fighting for your attention these days, but you chose to pick up a book. I'm not sure if you realize how rare and special that is nowadays. Time spent reading is never time wasted, and I dearly hope that you pick up another book very soon.

About the Author

Born and raised in Middle Tennessee, D. W. Gillespie wrote his first short story in second grade. It involved (unsurprisingly) monsters wreaking havoc on unsuspecting victims. Some things never change. He began writing seriously after taking a creative writing class in college, and he has been writing steadily ever since. He lives in Tennessee with his wife and two kids, and on dark nights, you might find them huddled around a campfire sharing spooky tales.

DWGILLESPIE.COM

Don't miss another
creepy read by

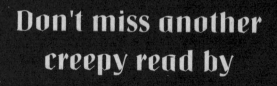

GRIN